"Well, what do you think of Zachary Thomas?"

Gramps blew a steady stream of smoke at the ceiling while he awaited her answer.

All afternoon, Janine had prepared herself for his question. Several complicated answers had presented themselves to her, clever replies that would sidestep her true feelings, but she used none of them now. Her grandfather expected the truth and it was her duty to give it to him. "I'm not exactly sure. He's not an easy man to know, is he?"

Anton chuckled. "No, he isn't. But Zachary will change," he said. "You're going to change him," he added after a thoughtful moment.

"Me?" Janine laughed outright at that. "I'm going to change Zachary Thomas?" she repeated in wide-eyed disbelief.

"Yes, you. You're going to teach him to laugh and enjoy life. But most important, you're going to teach him to love."

"I don't understand," Janine said, still confused. "I don't see where I come into this."

"I don't suppose you do," he said softly. "You see, Janine, I've cho___ ___ ___ your husband."

Debbie Macomber is an American writer born in the state of Washington, where she still lives. She and her electrician husband have four children, all of them teenagers. They also support a menagerie that includes horses, cats, a dog and some guinea pigs. Debbie's successful writing career actually started in childhood, when her brother copied—and sold—her diary! She's gone on to a considerably wider readership since then, as a prolific and popular author published in several different romance lines. She says she wrote her first book because she fell in love with Harlequin Romances—and wanted to write her own.

Books by Debbie Macomber

HARLEQUIN ROMANCE

FIRST
COMES MARRIAGE

Debbie Macomber

Harlequin Books

TORONTO • NEW YORK • LONDON
AMSTERDAM • PARIS • SYDNEY • HAMBURG
STOCKHOLM • ATHENS • TOKYO • MILAN

ISBN 0-373-03113-0

Harlequin Romance first edition March 1991

To Anna and Anton Adler,
Russian immigrants and
my loving grandparents.
Thank you for the wonderful heritage
you gave me.

FIRST COMES MARRIAGE

CHAPTER ONE

"YOU MUST BE Zachary Thomas," Janine said breathlessly as she whirled into the office. "I'm sorry I'm late, but I got hung up in traffic on Fourth Avenue. I didn't realize they'd torn up the whole street." Still a little winded, she unfastened her coat, tossed it over the back of the leather chair and plopped herself down, facing the large executive desk.

The man on the other side blinked twice as though he didn't quite know what to think.

"I'm Janine Hartman," she gasped out, flattening her hand over her chest. She drew in a deep steadying breath. "Gramps said if he wasn't back from his appointment, I should introduce myself."

"Yes," Zachary said after a moment of strained silence. "But he didn't tell me you'd be wearing—"

"Oh, the bandanna dress," Janine said, smoothing one hand over her lap. The entire dress had been constructed of red and blue bandannas; it featured a knee-length zigzag hemline and closely hugged her hips. "It was a gift. And since I'm meeting the girl who made it later, I thought the least I could do was wear it."

"I see. And the necklace?"

Janine toyed with the colored Christmas-tree lights strung between large bright beads on a bootlace that dangled from her neck. "It's a bit outrageous, isn't it?

That was a gift, too. I think it's kind of cute, though. Don't you? Pamela is so clever.''

''Pamela?''

''A teenager from the Friendship Club.''

''I . . . see,'' Zach said, frowning.

''I do volunteer work there and the two of us hit it off the moment we met. Pam's mother doesn't live in the area and she's at that awkward age and needs a friend. For some reason she took a liking to me, which was fine because I think she's wonderful.''

''I see.''

Janine doubted that he did.

''The necklace is *different* I'll grant you,'' Zach was saying—which wasn't admitting to much. His dark eyes narrowed as he studied the multicolored bulbs.

Now that she'd met Zachary Thomas, Janine could understand why her grandfather was so impressed with him, if appearances were anything to judge by. In his well-tailored suit, he was the very picture of a high-powered executive, crisp, formal and in control. He was younger than she'd assumed, possibly in his early thirties, but it was difficult to tell. His facial features were attractive enough, she noted, but he wasn't strikingly handsome. Still, she found herself fascinated by the strength of character she saw in the uneven planes of his face. His dark hair was cut military short. His jaw was strong, his cheekbones high and his mouth full. That was the way she'd describe him physically, but there was apparently much more to the man than met the eye. At least, her grandfather was convinced of it.

Several months earlier Anton Hartman had merged his well-established business supply firm with the up-and-rising company owned by Zachary Thomas. Together the two men had quickly dominated the market.

For weeks now, Gramps had wanted Janine to meet Zachary. His name had popped up in every conversation, no matter what they were discussing. To say her grandfather thought highly of his partner was a gross understatement.

"Gramps has spoken...highly of you," she said next.

A hint of a smile—just the merest suggestion—touched the edges of his mouth, giving her the impression that he didn't smile often. "Your grandfather has one of the keenest business minds in the country."

"He's incredible, isn't he?"

Zachary's nod betrayed no hesitation.

There was a polite knock on the door, and almost immediately afterward, a tall middle-aged woman wearing a navy-blue pin-striped suit stepped into the room. "Mr. Hartman phoned," she announced primly. "He's been delayed and suggested you two meet him at the restaurant."

"I see." Zach's lean dark face tightened briefly before he cast Janine an uneasy glance. "Did he say how long he was going to be?"

"I'm sorry, Mr. Thomas, but he didn't."

Janine glanced at her watch. She was scheduled to meet Pam at three. If they were delayed much longer, she'd be late.

She scowled at Zach's apparent reluctance to entertain her in Gramp's absence. "Maybe it would be best if we rescheduled lunch for another day," she offered brightly. She wasn't any happier about the prospect of waiting in a restaurant, just the two of them, than he was. "Gramps is held up, I'm meeting Pam later, and you're obviously a busy man."

An uncomfortable silence followed her remark. "Is it your habit not to show up when your grandfather is expecting you?" he asked sharply.

Janine bristled. "Of course not." She swallowed the words to defend herself. Her suggestion hadn't been unreasonable and he had no right to insinuate that she was inconsiderate and rude.

"Then I suggest we meet your grandfather at the restaurant as he requested," he finished stiffly.

"By all means," she said, forcing a smile. She stood and reached for her coat, watching Zach from the corner of her eye. He didn't like her. The realization had a peculiar effect on Janine. She felt disappointed and a little sad. Zach hadn't said much, and actually there hadn't been time for a real conversation, but she'd sensed his attitude almost from the first. He thought of her as spoiled and frivolous, probably because he knew she didn't hold a responsible job and loved to travel. Part of her longed to explain that there were good reasons she'd chosen the life-style she had. But from the looks he was giving her, it would be a waste of breath to justify herself.

Besides, it was more important to maintain the peace, however strained, for Gramps's sake, Janine decided. She'd have enjoyed getting to know Zach, perhaps even becoming friends, but that didn't seem likely. It was unfortunate, really.

That morning, before Gramps had left the house, he'd been as excited as a little boy about their luncheon date. He'd come down the stairs whistling when he'd joined her for breakfast, his blue eyes sparkling. When she'd refused the use of the limousine, he'd spent the next fifteen minutes giving her detailed directions, as though she'd never driven in downtown Seattle.

Almost as an afterthought, he'd mentioned that he had a morning meeting with an important client. If he hadn't returned by the time she arrived, she was to go directly to Zach's office, introduce herself and wait for him there.

Shrugging into a raincoat, Zachary moved toward the door. "Are you ready?"

She nodded, burying her hands in her pockets.

Thankfully the restaurant her grandfather had chosen was close by. By tacit agreement, they began to walk the few short blocks, although Janine had trouble matching her stride with Zach's much longer one.

Struggling to keep up with him, Janine studied Zachary Thomas, trying to determine exactly what disturbed her about the man. His height was a good example. He wasn't tall—under six feet, she guessed—and since she was almost five-eight there wasn't more than a few inches' difference between them. Why, then, did he make her feel much shorter?

He must have sensed her scrutiny because he turned and glared at her. Janine offered him a feeble smile, and felt the color rise in her cheeks. Zach's quick dismissive glance did nothing to boost her ego. She wasn't vain, but Janine knew she was attractive. Over the years, plenty of men had told her so, including Brian, the man who'd broken her heart. But she could have warts on her nose for all the notice Zachary Thomas gave her.

If he found the bandanna dress disconcerting, then he was probably put off by her hairstyle as well. She wore it short, neatly trimmed in the back with extra-long bangs slanted across her forehead. For years Janine had worn her hair shoulder-length, parted in the middle. One afternoon a few weeks earlier, for no particular reason, she'd decided to have it cut. She was in the mood for something radical and the style she now sported seemed more appropriate to the pages of a fashion magazine. Pam had been crazy about the change, insisting she looked phenomenal. Janine wasn't convinced. Her one comfort was that, given time, the thick dark length would return.

Janine suspected Zach had characterized her as flamboyant, if not downright flashy. She in turn would describe him as austere and disciplined, perhaps solitary. Her grandfather saw all that, she knew, and a good deal more.

"Mr. Hartman is waiting for you," the maître d' informed them when they arrived at the plush waterfront restaurant. He led them across the thick carpet to a high semi-circular booth upholstered in blue velvet.

"Janine, Zach." Anton Hartman smiled broadly as they approached. The years had been good to her grandfather. His bearing was still straight and confident, though his hair had grown completely white. His deep blue eyes, only a little faded, were filled with warmth, and wisdom. "I apologize for the inconvenience."

"It wasn't any problem," Zach answered for both of them before Janine could respond—as if he'd expected her to complain!

Ignoring him, Janine removed her coat and kissed her grandfather's leathery cheek with affection.

"Janine," he began, then gasped. "Where did you ever get that . . . dress?"

"Do you like it?" She threw out her arms and whirled around once to give him the full effect. "I know it's a bit unconventional, but I didn't think you'd mind."

Gramps's gaze flickered to Zach, then back to her. "On anyone else it would be scandalous, but on you, my dear, it's a work of art."

"Honestly, Gramps," she said, laughing softly. "You never could lie very well." She slid into the booth next to her grandfather, forcing him into the center, between her and Zach. Gramps looked a bit disgruntled, but after her turbulent first encounter with Zach, she preferred to keep her distance from the man. For that matter, he didn't seem all that eager to be close to her, either.

She glanced at him and noted, almost smugly, that he was already studying the menu. No doubt he found ordinary conversation a waste of time. Janine reached for her own menu. She was famished. At breakfast, she'd only had time for coffee and a single piece of toast, and she had every intention of making up for it now.

When the waiter came to take their order, Janine asked for the seafood entrée and soup *and* salad. She'd decide about dessert later, she said. Once he'd left, Gramps leaned toward Zach. "Janine never has to worry about her weight." He made this sound as if it was a subject of profound and personal interest to them both. "Her grandmother was the same way. How my Anna could eat, and she never gained an ounce. Janine's just like her."

"Gramps," Janine whispered under her breath. "I'm sure Zach couldn't care one way or the other how much I weigh."

"Nonsense," Gramps said and gently patted her hand. "I hope you two had the chance to introduce yourselves."

"Oh yes." Janine returned automatically.

"Your granddaughter is everything you claimed," Zachary said, but the inflection in his voice suggested something entirely different to Janine than it did to her grandfather. She guessed that to Anton, he seemed courteous and complimentary. But he was telling Janine he'd found her to be the spoiled darling he'd long suspected. He didn't openly dislike her, but he wasn't too impressed with her, either.

Unfortunately, that was probably due to more than just the dress and the lightbulb necklace.

Janine watched for her grandfather's reaction to Zach's words and she knew she was right when his gaze warmed and he nodded, obviously pleased by his partner's assessment. Zachary Thomas was clever, Janine had to grant him that much.

"How did the meeting with Anderson go?" Zach asked.

For a moment her grandfather stared at him blankly. "Oh, Anderson... Fine, fine. Everything went just as I'd hoped." Then he cleared his throat and carefully spread the linen napkin across his lap. "As you both know," he said, "I've been wanting the two of you to meet for some time now. Janine is the joy of my life. She's kept me young and brought me much happiness over the years. I fear that, without her, I would have turned into a bitter old man."

His look was so full of tenderness that Janine had to lower her eyes and swallow back a rush of tears. Gramps had been her salvation too. He'd taken her in after the deaths of her parents, raised her with a gentle hand and loved her enough to allow her to be herself. It must have been difficult for him to have a six-year-old unexpectedly thrust into his life, but he'd never complained.

"My only son died far too young," Anton admitted slowly, painfully.

"I'm sorry," Zachary murmured.

The genuine compassion Janine heard in his voice surprised her. And it definitely pleased her. Zach's respect and affection for her grandfather won her immediate approval—even if the man didn't seem likely to ever feel anything so positive toward *her*.

"For many years I mourned the loss of my only child," Anton continued, his voice gaining strength. "I've worked all my life, built an empire that stretches across these fifty states, and in the process have become a wealthy man."

Janine studied her grandfather closely. He was rarely this serious. He wasn't one to list his accomplishments, and she wondered at his strange mood.

"When Zach brought his business into the area, I saw in him a rare gift, one that comes along seldom in life. It's said that there are men in this world who make things happen, those who watch things happen, and then those who wonder what happened. Zachary is a man who makes things happen. In many ways, the two of us are alike. That's one of the primary reasons I decided to approach him with a proposal to merge our companies."

"I'm honored that you should think so, sir."

"Sir," Anton repeated softly and chuckled. He raised his hand, motioning for the waiter. "You haven't called me that in six months, and there's no reason to start again now."

The waiter returned with a bottle of expensive French champagne. Soon glasses were poured and set before them.

"Now," Anton continued, "as I said earlier, I have the two people I love most in this world together with me for the first time, and I don't mind telling you, it feels good." He raised his glass. "To happiness."

"Happiness," Janine echoed, sipping her champagne. Her eyes met Zach's above the crystal flute and she saw a glint of admiration. If she were dining on it, she'd starve—to quote a favorite expression of her grandfather's—but it was just enough for her to know he would think kindly of her because of her love for Anton.

Her grandfather chuckled and whispered something in his native tongue, a German dialect from the old country. Over the years she'd picked up a smattering of the language, but when she'd repeated a few phrases to a college German professor, he'd barely recognized the words. Gramps paused and his gaze lingered on Janine, then went to Zach. Whatever Gramps was muttering appeared to please him. His blue eyes fairly twinkled with delight.

"And now," he said, setting his glass aside. "I have an important announcement to make."

He looked to Janine and his face softened with deep affection. "I feel as though I've been an impossible burden to you, child, what with running this company," he said thoughtfully. "Never in all my dreams did I expect to accumulate so much in a single lifetime. I realize I've stayed in the business far longer than I should. It's time for me to retire and do a little traveling."

"It's past time," Janine argued. For years, she'd been urging her grandfather to lessen his heavy work schedule. He'd often spoken of revisiting his birth-place and the surrounding countries. He talked at length of cousins and friends he'd left behind in the small German settlement in what was now part of the Soviet Union.

"This is where Zachary comes into the picture," Anton explained. "I know myself all too well. Full retirement would be impossible for me. If I stopped working, I'd shrivel up and die. That's just the way I am," he said simply.

Neither Janine nor Zachary disputed his words.

"I'll never be able to keep my fingers out of the business, yet I want to enjoy my travels. I couldn't do that if I was fretting about what was happening at the home office." He paused as if he expected one of them to contradict him. "I believe I've come upon a solu-tion. As of this afternoon, Zachary, I'm handing over the reins to you. You will assume my position as chairman of the board. I realize this is sooner than we discussed, but the time is right and I hope you'll agree."

"But, Anton—"

"Gramps—"

Anton held up his hand. "I've thought about this long and hard," he said confidently. "I find Zach's honesty unquestionable, his loyalty certain and his intelligence keen. He's shrewd, perceptive and in-sightful. I know of no better man, and there's no bet-ter time."

Janine studied Zach, and she noted that he seemed uncomfortable with the praise. "Thank you," was all he said.

"A share of this company will belong to you some-day, Janine," Anton said next. "Do you have any objections to this appointment?"

She opened her mouth, but nothing came out. Of course she approved. What else could she do? "Whatever you decide is fine with me."

Anton turned his attention to the other man. "Zachary do you accept?"

Although their acquaintance had been brief, Janine knew instinctively that it took a lot to fluster this man. But her grandfather had managed to do so.

Zachary continued to stare at him as though he couldn't quite believe what he was hearing. But when he spoke, his voice was well modulated, revealing little of his emotions. "I'm honored."

"For the next few months, we'll be working closely together, much as we have in the past, but with a difference. No longer will I be teaching you the ropes. I'll be giving them to you."

The first course of their luncheon order arrived, and to Janine's delight, the conversation flowed smoothly. Her grandfather made sure of that. He was jubilant and entertaining, witty and charming. It would have been impossible not to be affected by his good humor.

When they'd finished the meal, Zachary glanced at his watch, his look regretful. "I'm sorry to leave so soon, but I have an appointment."

Janine noted the time and took a last sip of her coffee. "I should be leaving, too." She reached for her purse and coat, then slid out of the booth, waiting for her grandfather to join her.

"If neither of you objects, I'm going to linger over my coffee," Anton said, nodding toward the steaming cup.

"Of course." Janine leaned over to kiss him good-bye.

Zachary walked out to the street with her. Before he left, he shook her hand. "It's been a pleasure, Miss Hartman."

"You're sure?" she teased, unable to stop herself.

"Yes." His eyes held hers and he bestowed on her what she suspected was a rare smile. She walked away feeling oddly excited about their meeting. Zach wasn't an easy person to know, but she had the impression that he was everything her grandfather claimed and more.

GRAMP'S MOOD remained cheerful when he arrived home later that evening. Janine was in the library sipping herbal tea with her feet tucked under her as she watched the local news.

Sitting down in the wingback leather chair next to her, Gramps crossed his legs and reached for one of his Havana cigars. Janine watched him light it and shook her head affectionately; she loved her grandfather dearly and wished he'd stop smoking, though she no longer bothered to express that wish. He was the kind of man who did exactly as he chose, got exactly what he wanted. He was obviously pleased with the way their luncheon had gone, and she wondered briefly if Zach had said anything about her afterward. Somehow she doubted it.

"Well," he said after a moment, "What do you think of Zachary Thomas?" He blew a steady stream of smoke at the ceiling while he awaited her answer.

All afternoon, Janine had prepared herself for his question. Several complicated answers had presented themselves to her, clever replies that would sidestep her true feelings, but she used none of them now. Her grandfather expected the truth, and it was her duty to give it to him.

"I'm not exactly sure. He's not an easy man to know, is he?"

Anton chuckled. "No, he isn't, but I've never known you to walk away from a challenge. The boy's a little rough around the edges, but on the inside, he's pure gold."

Janine hadn't thought of Zach in those terms—a challenge. Frankly, she doubted there would be much reason for her to have any future contact with him. Gramps and Zach would be working closely together, but she had little if anything to do with the business.

"I've earned his trust, but it took time," Gramps was saying now.

"I'm glad you've decided to retire," she said absently, half listening to the weather report.

"Zachary will change," her grandfather added.

He had her full attention now. "Gramps," she said patiently, holding in a laugh. "Why should he? He's achieved considerable financial success. Everything's looking good for him. What possible reason could there be for him to change?"

Before Anton answered, he stood and poured himself a liberal dose of brandy, swirling it slowly in the bottom of the snifter. "You're going to change him," he said after a thoughtful moment.

"Me?" Janine laughed outright. "I'm going to change Zachary Thomas?" she repeated in wide-eyed disbelief. That would be the day!

"Before you argue with me, and I can see that's what you're dying to do, I have a story I want to tell you. A rather sad one as it happens."

Janine picked up the remote control and snapped off the television. She'd often listened to grandfather's parables. "So tell me."

"It's about a boy, born on the wrong side of the tracks to an alcoholic father and a weak mother. He never had much of a chance in life. His father was abusive enough for the state to remove the lad and his younger sister from the home. He was barely eight and subjected to a long series of foster homes, but he refused to be separated from his sister. He'd promised her he'd always be there to take care of her.

"Once there wasn't any alternative and the two were placed in separate homes. Beside himself with worry for his sister, the young boy ran away. The authorities were in a panic, but three days later, he turned up two hundred miles away at the home where they'd placed Beth Ann."

"He probably felt responsible for her."

"Yes. Which made matters much worse when she drowned in a swimming accident when he was twelve."

"Oh, no." A pain squeezed Janine's heart at the agony the boy had suffered at the death of his sister.

"He blamed himself, of course," Anton said softly.

"The poor kid."

"This lad never seemed to belong to anyone after that," Gramps continued, staring into his brandy. "He never quite fit in, but that wasn't entirely his fault." He paused to take another puff on his cigar. "His mother died a month after his sister. They were the only ones who had ever truly loved the boy. He lost contact with his father, which was probably for the best. So his family was gone and no one seemed to want this troubled, hurting youth."

"Did he turn into a juvenile delinquent?" It made sense to Janine that he would; she'd dealt with several troubled teenagers through her volunteer work and was familiar with tragic patterns that so often evolved, in cases like this.

"No, I can't say that he did." Gramps dismissed her question with a short shake of his head, more interested in continuing his tale than getting sidetracked by her questions. "He drifted through childhood without an anchor and without ever being allowed to enjoy those early formative years."

"Gramps—"

He raised his hand to stop her. "When this lad was eighteen, he joined the military. He did well, which isn't surprising, considering his intelligence and the fact that he held little regard for his own well being. There was no one to mourn if he died. Because of his courage, he advanced quickly, volunteering for the riskiest assignments. He traveled all over the world to some of the most dangerous political hot spots. His duties were often top secret. There's no telling how far he might have gone had he chosen to remain in the armed services, but for some reason, he resigned. No one understood why. I suspect he wanted to start his life over. This was when he opened a business-supply company. Within a year, he had my attention. His methods were aggressive and creative. I couldn't help admiring the way he handled himself and the company. Within five years, he'd become one of my most serious rivals. I saw a strength in him that age had stolen from me. We met. We talked. As a result of these talks we joined forces."

"Obviously you're telling me about Zachary's life."

Anton grinned and slowly sipped his brandy. "You discovered his remoteness quickly. I thought knowing all this would help you. Zach's never had the security that a caring home and family provide. He's never really experienced love, except what he shared with his sister, Beth Ann. His life has been a long progression of painful experiences. By sheer force of will, he's managed to overcome every obstacle placed in his path. I realize Zachary Thomas isn't going to win any Mr. Personality contests, but by heaven, he's earned my respect."

Janine had rarely heard such emotion in her grandfather's voice. "Zach told you all this?"

Anton's quick burst of laughter echoed through the room. "You're joking, aren't you? Zach has never spoken of his past to me. I doubt that he has to anyone."

"You had him investigated?"

Gramps puffed on his cigar before answering. "It was necessary, although I'd guessed early on that his life hadn't been a bed of roses."

"It's all very sad, isn't it?"

"You're going to be very good for him, my dear."

Janine blinked. "Me?"

"Yes, you. You're going to teach him to laugh and enjoy life. But most important, you're going to teach him love."

She hesitated, uncertain of her grandfather's meaning. "I don't think I understand. I realize Zach and I will probably be seeing each other now and again since he's assuming your responsibilities with the company, but I don't see how I could have any great impact on his life."

Gramps smiled, a slow lazy smile that curved up the corners of his mouth. "That's where you're wrong, my dear. You're going to play a very big role in Zach's life, and he in yours."

Janine was still confused. "Perhaps I missed something this afternoon. I thought you made Zach the chairman of the board."

"I did." A lazy swirl of smoke circled his white head.

"I don't understand where I come into the picture."

"I don't suppose you do," he said softly. "You see, Janine, I've chosen Zachary to be your husband."

CHAPTER TWO

FOR A STUNNED MOMENT, Janine said and did nothing. "You're teasing, aren't you, Gramps?"

"No," he said, lighting a second cigar. He paused to stare at the glowing tip, his eyes filled with mischief—and with something else, less easily defined. "I'm dead serious."

"But..." Janine's thoughts were so jumbled she couldn't make sense of them herself, let alone convey her feelings to her grandfather.

"I've been giving the matter serious consideration for some time now. Zach's perfect for you and you're the ideal complement to him. You're going to have beautiful blond-haired children."

"But..." Janine discovered she was absolutely speechless. One minute she was listening to a touching parable, and the next her grandfather was telling her about the husband he'd arranged for her and the color of her children's hair.

"Once you think about it," Gramps continued confidently, "I'm sure you'll agree with me. Zach is a fine young man, and he'll make you an excellent husband."

"You...Zach talked...agreed?" The words stumbled over the end of her tongue like toppling building blocks.

"Do you mean have I suggested this arrangement to Zach?" Gramps asked. "Heavens, no. At least not yet." He chuckled as if he found the mere thought amusing. "Zach wouldn't appreciate my blatant interference in his personal affairs. With him, I'll need to be far more subtle. To be honest, I considered making this marriage part of my handing over the chairmanship, but after thinking matters through, I changed my mind. Zach would never have agreed to it. There are other ways, I decided, better ways. But I don't want you to worry about it. That's between Zach and me."

"I . . . see." At this point, Janine wasn't sure *what* she saw, other than one determined old man caught between two worlds. In certain respects, the old ways continued to dominate his thinking, but his success in America allowed him to appreciate more modern outlooks.

Gramps inhaled deeply on his cigar, his blue eyes twinkling. "Now, I realize you probably find the idea of an arranged marriage slightly unorthodox, but you'll get used to it. I've made a fine choice for you, and I know you're smart enough to recognize that."

"Gramps, I don't think you fully understand what you're suggesting," she said, trying to gather her scattered thoughts, hoping to find a way of explaining the ridiculousness of this whole scheme without offending him.

"But I do, my child."

"In this country and in this age," she continued slowly, "men and women choose their own mates. We fall in love and then marry."

Gramps frowned. "Sadly, that doesn't work," he muttered.

"What do you mean, it doesn't work?" she cried, losing her patience. "It's been that way for years and years!"

"Look at the divorce rate. I read in the newspaper recently that almost fifty percent of all marriages in this country fail. In the old country, there was no divorce. Parents decided whom a son or daughter would marry, and their decision was accepted without question. First comes marriage, and then comes love."

"Gramps," Janine said softly, wanting to reason this out with him. Her grandfather was a logical man; surely if she explained it properly, he'd understand. "Things are done differently now. First comes love, then comes marriage."

"What do you young people know about love?"

"A good deal, as it happens," she returned, lying smoothly. Her first venture into the emotion had ended in a broken heart and a shattered ego, but Gramps knew little if anything about Brian.

"Pfft!" he spat. "What could you possibly know of love?"

"I realize," she said, thinking fast, "your father arranged your marriage to Grandma, but that was years ago, and in America such customs don't exist. You and I live here now, in the land of the free. The land of opportunity."

Gramps gazed down into his brandy for a long moment, lost in thought. Janine doubted he'd even heard her.

"I'll never forget the first time I saw my Anna," he said in a faraway voice that was haunting and gentle. "She was sixteen and her hair was long and blond and fell in braids all the way to her waist. My father spoke to her father and while they were talking, Anna and I sat at opposite ends of the room from each other, too shy to look at each other. I wondered if she thought I was handsome. To me, she was the most beautiful girl in the world. Even now, after all these years, I can remember how my heart beat with excitement when I first saw her. I knew—''

''But Gramps that was nearly sixty years ago! Marriages aren't decided by families any longer. A man and a woman discover each other without a father introducing them. Maybe the old ways were better back then, but it's simply not done like that anymore.'' Gramps continued to stare into his glass, lost in a world long since enveloped by the passage of time.

''The next day, Anna's parents visited our farm and again our two fathers spoke. I tried to pretend I wasn't concerned, determined to accept whatever our families decided. But when I saw our fathers shake hands and slap each other on the back, I knew Anna would soon be mine.''

''You loved her before you were married, didn't you?'' Janine asked softly, hoping to prove her point.

''No,'' he returned flatly, without hesitation, ''How could I love her when I'd only seen her twice before the wedding ceremony? We hadn't said more than a handful of words to each other. Love wasn't necessary for us to find happiness. Love came later, after we arrived in America.''

''Wasn't it unusual for a marriage to be arranged even then?'' There had to be some point for her to contend, Janine mused.

''Perhaps in other parts of the world, but not in Vibiskgrad. We were a small farming community. Our world had been ravaged by war and hate. We clung to each other, holding on to our own traditions and rituals. Soon our lives became impossible and we were forced to flee our homes."

"As I said before, I can understand how an arranged marriage—back then—might be the best for everyone involved. But I can't see it working in this day and age. I'm sorry to disappoint you, Gramps, but I'm not willing to accept Zachary Thomas as my husband, and I'm sure he would be equally unwilling to marry me."

Briefly Gramps's face tensed with a rare display of disappointment and indignation, then quickly relaxed. Janine had seldom questioned his authority and had never openly defied him.

"I suppose this idea is a shock to you, isn't it?" he said.

If it astonished her, she couldn't wait to hear what Zachary Thomas thought! They'd only met once, but he hadn't disguised his opinion of her. He wouldn't take kindly to Gramps's plan of an arranged marriage—especially to a woman he viewed as spoiled and overindulged.

"All I'm asking is that you consider this, Janine," Gramps said, breaking into her thoughts. "Promise me you'll at least do that. Don't reject marriage to Zach simply because you consider it old-fashioned."

"Oh, Gramps..." Janine hated to refuse him anything. "It isn't just me. What about Zach? What about *his* plans? What if he—"

Gramps dismissed her questions with an abrupt shrug. "How often do I ask something of you?", he persisted.

Now he was going to use guilt. "Not often," she agreed, frowning at him for using unfair tactics.

"Then consider Zach for your husband!" His eyes brightened. "The two of you will have such beautiful children. A grandfather knows these things."

"I promise I'll think about it." But it wouldn't do any good! However, discretion was a virtue Janine was nurturing, and there had never been a better time than now to employ it.

GRAMPS DIDN'T MENTION Zach Thomas or even hint at the subject of her marrying his business partner again until the following evening. They'd just sat down to dinner, prepared to sample Mrs. Mc-Cormick's delicious fare, when Gramps looked anxiously at Janine. "So?" he asked breathlessly.

From the moment he'd walked into the house that afternoon, Gramps's mood had been light and humorous. He was grinning now as he handed her the platter of thinly sliced marinated and grilled flank steak. It happened to be one of Janine's favorite meals. "So?" he repeated, smiling at her. "What did you decide?"

Janine helped herself to a crisp dinner roll, taking her time buttering it while her thoughts chased each other in frantic circles. "Nothing."

His smile collapsed into a frown. "You promised me you'd consider marrying Zach. I gave you more time than Anna's father gave her."

"You have to know now?"

"Now!"

"But, Gramps, a simple yes or no doesn't answer something as complex as this. You're asking me to decide on a lifelong commitment in less than twenty-four hours." She was stalling for time, and Gramps had probably guessed as much. Frankly, she didn't know what to tell him. She couldn't, wouldn't, marry Zach—even if he was willing to marry her—but at the same time she hated disappointing her grandfather.

"What's so difficult? Either you marry him, or not."

"I don't understand why you've decided to match me up with Zach Thomas," she cried. "What's wrong with Peter?" She'd been dating the other man casually for the last few months. Her heart was too bruised after what had happened with Brian for her to consider dating anyone seriously.

"You're in love with that whitewashed weakling, that..."

Janine signed loudly, regretting the fact she'd introduced Peter into their conversation. "He's very nice."

"So is chocolate mousse!" Gramps muttered. "Peter Donahue would make you a terrible husband. I'm shocked you'd even consider marrying him."

"I hadn't actually thought about him in those terms," she clarified. Peter was witty and fun, but Gramps was right; they weren't suited as husband and wife.

"I thank the good Lord you've been given some sense."

Janine took a deep breath and finally asked a question that had been nagging at her all afternoon. "Did—did you arrange my father's marriage?"

Gramps lowered his eyes, but not before he could disguise the pain there. "No. He fell in love with Patrice while he was in college. I knew from the first that the match wasn't a good one, but Anna reminded me this was America and young people fell in love by themselves. She convinced me they didn't need a father's guiding hand the way we did in the old country."

"Do you think he would have listened if you'd wanted to arrange a marriage?"

Her grandfather hesitated, and his hand tightened on the water glass. "I don't know, but I'd like to think he would have."

"Instead he married my mother."

Neither spoke for a long moment. Janine remembered little of her parents, only bits and pieces of memories, mostly unconnected. What she did recall were terrible fights and accusations, a house filled with strife. She could remember hiding under her bed when the shouting started, pressing her hands to her ears. It was her father who used to find her, who comforted her. Always her father. Her memory included little of her mother. Even pictures didn't jar her recollection, although Janine had spent hour upon hour looking at the photographs, hoping to remember something. But the woman who had given birth to her had remained a stranger to her in life and in death.

"You're the only consolation I have from Steven's marriage," Anton said hoarsely. "At least Steven and Patrice gave you to me before they died."

"Oh, Gramps. I love you so much and I hate with everything that's in me to disappoint you, but I can't marry Zach and, frankly, I can't see him agreeing to marry me."

Her grandfather quieted after that, seeming to mull over her words as he finished his dinner. "I suppose I seem like a feeble old man, still trying to live in the old ways."

"Gramps, no, I don't think that at all."

He planted his elbows squarely on the table and linked his fingers, gazing at her. His brow was puckered in a contemplative frown. "Perhaps it would help me understand if you told me what you want in a husband."

She hesitated, then glanced away, avoiding eye contact. Once she'd been so certain of what she wanted. "To be perfectly honest, I'm not sure. Romance, I suppose."

"Romance." Slowly Gramps rolled the word off his tongue as though it were an expensive delicately flavored wine.

"Yes," she said with a hard nod of her head, gaining confidence.

"And exactly what is romance?"

"Well . . ." Now that she'd been called upon to define it, Janine wasn't sure she could put that magical feeling into words. "It's an awareness that comes from the heart."

"The heart," her grandfather repeated, smacking his palm against his chest.

"Romance is the knowledge that a man would rather die than live his life without me," she said, warming to the subject.

"You want him to die?"

"No, just be willing."

Gramps frowned. "I don't think I understand."

"Romance is forbidden trysts on lonely Scottish moors," she added, thinking of an historical romance she'd read as a teenager.

"There aren't any moors in the Seattle area."

"Don't distract me," she said, smiling, her thoughts gaining momentum. "Romance is desperate passion."

"That sounds more like hormones to me."

"Gramps, please!"

"How can I understand when all you say is ridiculous things? You want romance. First you claim it's a feeling in the heart, then you say it's some kind of passion."

"It's more than that. It's walking hand in hand along the beach at twilight and gazing into each other's eyes. It's speaking of love without ever having to say the words." She paused, feeling a little foolish at getting so carried away. "I don't know that I can adequately describe it. I don't think anyone can."

"That's because you haven't experienced it."

"Maybe not," she agreed reluctantly. "But I will someday."

"With Zach," he said with complete assurance and a wide grin.

Janine didn't bother to argue anymore. Gramps was being obstinate and arguing with him was pointless. The only recourse she had was time itself. Soon enough he'd realize that neither she nor Zach was going to willingly fall in with his scheme. Then, and only then, would he drop the subject.

A WEEK PASSED and Gramps hadn't mentioned another word about arranging a marriage between her and Zachary Thomas. It was a cold windy March evening and the rain was coming down in torrents. Janine loved nights like this and was curled up in her favorite chair with a mystery novel when the doorbell chimed. Gramps had gone out for the evening and she wasn't expecting anyone.

She turned on the porch light, and looked out the peephole to discover Zach standing there, a briefcase clenched in his hand. His shoulders were hunched against the pelting rain.

"Zach," she said in surprise, throwing open the door.

"Hello, Janine," he said politely, stepping inside the house. "Is your grandfather here?"

"No." She pressed the novel against her chest, her heart pounding hard and fast. "He went out."

Zach frowned, clearly confused. "He asked me to stop by. There were some business matters he wanted to discuss. Did he say when he'd be returning home?"

"No, but I'm sure if he asked you over, then it'll be soon. Would you care to wait for him?"

"Please."

She took his raincoat and led him into the library where she'd been reading. A gentle fire was burning, and its warmth hugged the room. The three-story house, situated in Seattle's Mt. Baker district, was a typical turn-of-the-century home with high ceilings and spacious rooms. The third floor had once housed several servants. Charles was their only live-in help now, and his quarters had always been an apartment over the carriage house. He worked exclusively for Gramps, driving the limousine. Mrs. McCormick arrived early in the mornings and was responsible for the housekeeping chores and meal preparation.

"Can I get you something to drink?" she asked, once he was comfortably seated.

"Coffee, if you have it."

"I made a fresh pot about twenty minutes ago."

Janine brought him a cup from the kitchen, then sat across from Zach, wondering what, if anything, she should say about Gramps and his idea of an arranged marriage.

She doubted that Gramps had approached him yet. Otherwise he wouldn't be sitting there so calmly sipping coffee. If Gramps had broached the subject, she was convinced Zach wouldn't appear nearly so serene. He'd be outraged and infuriated, and studying him now, she concluded that he wasn't even slightly ruffled. It was on the tip of her tongue to warn him about what was coming, but she decided against it. Better that he learn of Gramps's plans the same way she had.

Lacing her fingers together, she smiled, feeling awkward and a little gauche. "It's nice to see you again."

"You, too. I'll admit I'm a bit disappointed, though."

"You are?"

"On the drive over, I was trying to guess what you might be wearing this time. A dress made from bread sacks? A blouse constructed out of men's socks?"

She muttered under her breath, miffed by his teasing tone. He had the uncanny ability to make her feel fifteen all over again. So much for any possibility that they'd ever be compatible. And Gramps seemed to think he knew them both so well.

"I'll admit that an Irish cable-knit sweater and wool slacks are a pleasant surprise," he said.

A flicker of admiration sparked in his dark eyes, something that had been sadly missing the first time they'd met.

In that instant, Janine knew.

She went stock-still, almost dizzy with the realization. Not only had Gramps approached Zach, but they'd apparently reached some sort of agreement. Otherwise Zach would never have been this friendly, this openly appreciative of her charms. Nor would he arrive unannounced when Gramps had specifically stated that he'd be gone for the evening.

They were obviously plotting against her. Well, she had no intention of putting up with it. None. If Zach and Gramps thought they could lure her into marriage, they had a real surprise coming.

Squaring her shoulders she slid to the edge of her chair. "So you gave in to the pressure," she muttered, shooting him a scalding look. Unable to stay seated, she stormed to her feet and started pacing, rubbing her palms together as she cornered her thoughts. "Gramps got to you, didn't he?"

"I beg your pardon?" Zach stared up at her, his eyes wide and curious.

"And you agreed?" She slapped her hands against the sides of her legs and groaned, "I don't believe it, I simply don't believe it. I thought better of you than this."

"What don't you believe?"

"Of all the men I've met over the years, I would have sworn you were the type who'd refuse to be bought. I'm disappointed in you, Zach."

He remained calm and unperturbed, which infuriated her more than anything he could have said or done.

"I haven't the slightest idea what you're talking about," was all he said.

"Oh, sure, play the innocent," she snapped. She was so incensed that she continued to pace in heavy hurried steps. Standing still was impossible.

In response, Zach merely glanced at his watch and drank his coffee. "Does your grandfather know you suffer from these bouts of hysteria?"

"Funny, Zach, very funny."

He exhaled an exaggerated sigh. "All right, I'll take the bait. What makes you think I've been bought? By the way, before I forget, what exactly am I getting in exchange."

"Technically you're not getting anything, and I want that understood this very minute, because *I* refuse to be sold." Arms akimbo, she turned to glare down at him with the full force of her disdain. "What did he offer you? The entire company? Vast sums of money?"

Zach shrugged. "He's offered me nothing."

"Nothing," she repeated slowly, feeling unreasonably insulted. "He was just going to *give* me away." The realization was enough to deflate the billowing sails of her pride. Stunned, she sat back down in her chair. "I thought the bride's family was supposed to supply some kind of dowry. Gramps didn't even offer you money?"

"Dowry?" Zach repeated the word as if he'd never heard it before.

"Gramps's family received a cow and ten chickens for my grandmother," she said, as if that would explain everything. "But apparently I'm not even worth a single hen."

Zach set his coffee aside and sat straight in his chair. "I think we'd better begin this conversation again. I'm afraid I lost you back there when you said something about my cracking under pressure. Perhaps you should enlighten me about what I'm supposed to have done that's so terrible."

Janine just glared at him.

"Humor me."

"All right, if you insist. It's obvious that Gramps talked to you about the marriage."

"Marriage," he repeated in a shocked voice. His face went blank. "To whom?"

"Me, of course."

Zach flung himself out of the chair, bolting to his feet. "To you?"

"Don't look so horrified! My ego's taken about all it can for one evening. I'm not exactly the Wicked Witch of the West, you know. Some men would be more than happy to marry me." Not Brian, and certainly not Peter, but she felt it was important that Zach think she was sought after.

"Marriage between us is...would be impossible. It's completely out of the question. I don't ever plan to marry—I have no use for a wife or family."

"Tell that to Gramps."

"I have every intention of doing exactly that." His face tightened and Janine guessed her grandfather was due for an earful once he arrived. "What makes that crazy old man think he can order people's lives around like this?" he asked angrily.

"His marriage was arranged for him and for his father before him. Trust me, Zach, I argued until I was exhausted, but Gramps hasn't given up his old-country beliefs and he thinks the two of us—now this is really ridiculous—are perfect for each other."

"If you weren't so serious, I'd find this highly amusing."

Janine noticed that he seemed rather pale. "I appear to have jumped to conclusions earlier. I apologize for that but, well, I thought...I assumed Gramps had spoken to you already and you'd agreed."

"Was that when you started mumbling something about a cow and a few chickens?"

She nodded and her long bangs fell over her eyes. Absently she pushed them aside. "For a moment there, I thought Gramps was offering me to you gratis. I know it's silly, but I felt downright insulted by that."

For the first time since they'd entered into this conversation, Zach's face softened enough to grant her a faint smile. "Your grandfather loves you, no question."

"I know." Feeling self-conscious, she threaded her fingers through her hair. "I've used every argument I could come up with to combat this insane idea of his. I explained the importance of romance and told him how vital it was for men and women to fall in love with the person of their own choice. Apparently he doesn't accept that times have changed."

"He wouldn't listen to you?"

"He listened," she replied, feeling defeated, "but he disputed everything I said. Gramps claims the modern version of love and marriage is a complete failure. With the divorce rate what it is, I'm afraid I don't have much of an argument."

"That's true enough," Zach said, looking frustrated.

"I explained that men and women fall in love and then decide to marry, but Gramps insists it's better if marriage comes first."

"Dear Lord." Zach rubbed a hand over his face. "Now that I think about it, your grandfather has been introducing you into every conversation, telling me how wonderful you are."

Janine gasped softly. "He'd done the same to me about you, too, weeks before we even met."

Pressing his lips together, Zach nodded. "A lot of things are beginning to make sense."

"What are we to do?" Janine wondered aloud. "I mean, it's perfectly obvious we're going to have to agree on a plan of action. I hate to disappoint Gramps, but at the same time I'm not willing to be married off like...like..." Words failed her.

"Especially to me."

Although his low words were devoid of emotion, Janine recognized the pain behind his statement. Knowing what she did about his past, the fact that he'd experienced only brief patches of love in his life and little or no approval tugged at her heart.

"I didn't mean it to sound like that," she insisted. "My grandfather wouldn't have chosen you if he didn't think you were pretty special. He prides himself on his ability to judge character, and from the first, he's been impressed with you."

"Let's not kid ourselves, Janine," Zach returned, his voice hardening. "You're an uptown girl. We're about as suited as satin and burlap."

"I agree with you there, but not for the reasons you think. From the minute I stepped into your office, you made it clear you thought of me as some kind of snob. I'm not, but I refuse to waste my breath arguing with you."

"Fine."

"Instead of hurling insults at each other," she suggested tightly, crossing her arms in a show of indignation, "why don't we come up with a plan that will counter Gramps's preposterous idea?"

"That isn't necessary," he countered. "I'm not willing."

"And you think I am?"

Zach said nothing.

Janine expelled her breath with as much force as she could. "It seems to me the perfect solution is for one of us to marry someone else. That would quickly put an end to this whole thing."

"I already told you I have no intention of marrying," he said emphatically. "You're the one who insinuated you had plenty of men hanging around just waiting for you to say 'I do.'"

"None that I'd honestly consider marrying, for heaven's sake," she grumbled. "Besides, I'm not currently in love with anyone."

Zach laughed, if the sound that came from his throat could be called a laugh. "Then find a man who's current. If you fall in and out of love that easily, surely there's got to be at least one prospect on the horizon."

"There isn't. *You're* going to have to come up with someone! If you think you're such hot stuff, go out there and sweep some sweet young thing off her feet," she muttered sarcastically.

"I'm not willing to sacrifice my life so you can get off scot-free." His words were low and furious.

"But it's perfectly all right for *me* to sabotage mine. That makes a whole lot of sense."

"Okay," he said after a tense moment. He paused, raking one hand through his hair. "That idea's obviously not going to work. We'll have to come up with something better."

Janine gestured toward him. "It's your turn, bright boy."

He glared at her, seeming to dislike her even more. In all honesty, Janine wasn't too pleased with the way she was behaving, either. She'd been sarcastic and needlessly rude, but then, Zach had driven her to it. He could be the most unpleasant man.

Still Janine was about to say something concilia-tory when the sound of the front door opening dis-tracted her. Her gaze flew to Zach and he nodded, reassuring her he would handle this situation.

They returned to their chairs and were seated by the time Gramps appeared in the library doorway.

"Zach, I'm sorry for the delay. I'm pleased to see Janine entertained you." Her grandfather turned to-ward her with a bright smile as if to tell her he ap-proved and hoped she'd taken advantage of this time alone with Zach.

"We did manage to have a stimulating conversa-tion," Zach said, his eyes briefly linking with Ja-nine's.

"Good. Good."

Zach stood and reached for his briefcase. "There were some figures you wanted to go over with me?"

"Yes." Looking pleased with himself, Gramps led the way out of the room. Zach followed him, with a glance back at Janine that said he'd get in touch with her later.

Later turned out to be almost a week. She'd been puttering around outside, trimming back the rose-bushes and deciding where to plant the geraniums this year, when Mrs. McCormick came to tell her she was wanted on the phone.

"Hello," Janine said cheerfully.

"We need to talk," Zach said without preamble.

"Why?" she demanded. If he was going to keep her hanging for six anxious days, then she wasn't going to give the impression she was thrilled to hear from him.

"Your grandfather laid his cards on the table this afternoon. I thought you might be interested in hearing what he's offering me to take you off his hands."

CHAPTER THREE

"ALL RIGHT," Janine said, bracing herself. "What's he offering you? Huge bonuses?"

"No," Zach said quickly.

"Cash? I want to know exactly how much."

"He didn't offer me money."

Janine frowned. "What then?"

"I think we should meet and talk about it."

If her grandfather had openly approached Zach with the arranged-marriage idea, Janine knew darn well that Gramps would have made it worth Zach's while. Despite his impassioned claims to the contrary, it wouldn't have surprised Janine to discover that the newly appointed chairman of the board of Hartman-Thomas Business Supply had taken the bait.

"You want us to meet?" she repeated in a faltering voice.

"There's a good Italian restaurant on University Way—Italian 642. Have you heard of it?"

"No, but I'll find it."

"Good. Meet me there at seven." Zach paused, then added, "And listen, it might not be a good idea to let your grandfather know we're meeting. He might misunderstand our getting together."

"Right," Janine agreed.

Zach hesitated once more. "We have a lot to discuss."

Janine's heartbeat accelerated, and she felt the perspiration break out on her forehead. "Zach," she began, needing to know, "you haven't changed your mind, have you? I mean, you're not actually considering this ridiculous idea of his? You can't... We agreed, remember?" She swiped at her forehead with the back of her free hand as she waited for him to answer.

"You don't have anything to worry about," he finally said.

Replacing the telephone receiver, Janine had the sudden horrible sensation of being completely at her grandfather's mercy. He was an unshakably stubborn man who almost always got what he wanted through sheer determination. Faced with a mountain, Anton Hartman either climbed it, tunneled through it or forged a path around it; failing such active alternatives, he settled down in the foothills and waited for the mountain to dissolve. He claimed he won a majority of his battles by simply displaying patience. Janine called it not knowing when to pack up and go home.

She knew her grandfather's methods, but then so did Zach. But she hoped Anton's candidate for her husband would at least have the internal fortitude to withstand a few bribes, however tempting. Apparently he did, because he'd told her she had nothing to worry about. Yet on the other hand he sounded downright eager to discuss the subject with her.

"He *says* he never wants to marry," she muttered aloud in an effort to reassure herself. Indeed, Zachary Thomas was the last man Janine could imagine humming "The Wedding March"—especially when someone else was directing the band.

Janine was waiting in the library, coat draped over her arm, when her grandfather arrived home at six-thirty. He kissed her dutifully on the cheek and reached for the evening newspaper, scanning the headlines as he settled into his comfortable leather chair.

"Zach called," she said without thinking. She hadn't intended to mention that to Gramps.

Anton nodded. "I thought he might. You meeting him for dinner?"

"Dinner? Zach and me?" she squeaked. "No, of course not! Why would you even think I'd agree to a dinner date with...him?" Darn, how could she have nearly forgotten her promise to keep their meeting a secret? She detested lying to her grandfather, but there wasn't any help for it.

"But you are dining out?"

"Yes." She couldn't very well deny that, dressed as she was and carrying her coat.

"Then you're seeing Peter Donahue again?"

"No. Not exactly," Janine said uncomfortably, "I'm meeting a...friend."

"I see." The corners of Gramps's mouth quirked into a knowing smile.

Janine could feel the telltale heat saturating her face. She was a terrible liar, and always had been. Gramps knew as surely as if she'd spelled it out that she was meeting Zach. And when she told Zach she'd let it slip, he'd be furious with her, and rightly so.

"What did Zach want?"

"What makes you think he wanted anything?" Janine asked fervently. Her heart was thundering as she edged her way toward the door. The sooner she escaped, the better.

"You just said Zach phoned."

"Oh. Yes, he did, earlier, but it wasn't important. Something about...something." Brilliant! She rushed out of the house before Gramps could question her further. What a fool she was. Like a dunce she'd blurted out the very thing she'd wanted to keep secret.

By the time Janine located the Italian restaurant in the University district and found a parking place, she was ten minutes late.

Zach was sitting in a booth in the farthest corner of the room. He frowned when he saw her and glanced at his watch just so she'd know she'd kept him waiting.

Ignoring his disgruntled look, Janine slid onto the polished wooden bench, removed her coat and casually announced, "Gramps knows."

Zach's frown deepened. "What are you talking about."

"Gramps knows I'm having dinner with you," she explained. "I don't know what came over me. The minute he walked in the door, I told him you'd phoned—I just wasn't thinking—and when he asked why, I told him it had to do with *something*. I'm sure you'll be able to make up an excuse when he asks you later."

"I thought we agreed not to say anything about our meeting."

"I know," she said, feeling guiltier than ever. "But Gramps asked if I was going out with Peter and he just looked so smug when I told him I wasn't." At Zach's sudden movement, she burst out, "Well, what was I supposed to do?"

He grunted, which wasn't an answer one way or the other.

"If I wasn't going out with Peter, I'd have to come up with another man on the spot, and although I'm clever, I don't think that fast." She was breathless with frustration by the time she'd finished.

"Who's Peter?"

"This guy I've dated off and on for the past few months."

"And you're in love with him?"

"No, I'm not." Doubtless Zach would suggest she simply marry Peter and put an end to all this annoyance. Splendid idea.

Zach reached abruptly for the menu. "Let's order, and while we're eating we can go over what we need to discuss."

"All right," Janine agreed, grateful to leave the topic of her blunder. Besides, seven was later than she normally dined, and she was famished.

The waitress appeared then, and even as she filled Janine's water glass, her appreciative gaze never strayed from Zach. Once more Janine was struck by the knowledge that although he wasn't handsome in the traditional sense, he seemed to generate a good deal of female interest.

"I'll have the clam spaghetti," Janine said loudly, eyeing the attractive waitress, who seemed to be forgetting why she was there. The woman appeared far more interested in studying Zach than in taking their order.

"I'll have the same," Zach said, smiling briefly at the waitress as he handed her his menu. "Now, what were you saying?" he asked, returning his attention to Janine.

"As I recall, you were the one who insisted we meet. Just tell me what my grandfather said and be done with it." No doubt the offer had been generous; otherwise Zach wouldn't have suggested this dinner.

Zach's hand closed around the water glass. "Anton called me into his office to ask me a series of leading questions."

"Such as?"

Zach shrugged. "What I thought of you and—"

"How'd you answer him?"

Zach inhaled a deep breath. "I said I found you attractive, energetic, witty, a bit eccentric—"

"A bandanna dress and a string of Christmas tree lights doesn't make me eccentric," Janine insisted, her voice rising despite herself.

"If the Christmas tree lights are draped around your neck it does."

They were attracting attention, and after a few curious stares, Zach leaned closer and said, "If you're going to argue with everything I say, we'll be here all night."

"I'm sure our waitress would enjoy that," Janine snapped, then immediately regretted it. She sounded downright *jealous*—which, of course, was ridiculous.

"What are you talking about?"

"Never mind."

"Shall we return to the conversation between your grandfather and me?"

"Please," she said, properly chastised.

"Anton spent quite a long time telling me about your volunteer work at the Friendship Club and your various other community activities."

"No doubt his report was so glowing, I rank right up there with Joan of Arc and Florence Nightingale."

Zach grinned. "Something like that, but then he added that although you were constantly busy, he felt your life lacked contentment, purpose."

Janine could see it coming, as clearly as if she were standing on a track and a freight train was heading directly toward her. "Let me guess. He probably said I needed something more meaningful in my life—like a husband and children."

"Exactly." Zach nodded, his grin barely restrained. "In his opinion, marriage is the only thing that will fulfill you as woman."

Janine groaned and sagged against the back of her seat. It was worse than she thought. And to her chagrin, Zach actually looked amused by all this.

"You wouldn't look so smug if he claimed marriage was the only thing that would fulfill you as a *man*," she muttered. "Honestly, Zach, do I look like I'm wasting away from lack of purpose?" She gestured dramatically with her hands. "I'm happy, I'm busy...in fact I'm completely delighted with my life." It wasn't until she'd finished that she realized she was clenching her teeth.

"Don't take it so personally."

Janine rolled her eyes, wondering what his reaction would be if he were on the receiving end of this discussion.

"In case you didn't know it, your grandfather's a terrible chauvinist," he remarked, still smiling.

"Of course I know it, but he's so charming that it's easy to forgive him."

Zach reached for his wineglass and gazed at it thoughtfully. "What I can't figure out is why he's so keen on your marrying now. Why not last year? Or next year?"

"Heavens, I don't know. I suppose he thinks it's time. My biological clock's ticking away and the noise is probably keeping him awake nights. Heavens, by age twenty-four most of the women from the old country had four or five children."

"He certainly seems intent on the idea of marrying you off soon."

"Tell me about it!" Janine cried. "I'd bet cold cash that when he brought up the subject he insisted you were the only suitable man he'd found for me."

"Anton also said you have a generous heart, and that he feared some fast-talker would show up one day and turn your head."

"He said that?" she asked weakly. Her heart plowed to a dead stop, then jolted to life again. Anton's scenario sounded exactly like her disastrous romance with Brian. She sighed deeply. "So then he told you he wants me to marry someone he respects, someone he loves like a son. A man of discretion and wisdom and honor. A man he trusted enough to merge companies with."

Zach arched his brows. "You know your grandfather well."

"I can just imagine what came next," Janine added scathingly and her stomach clenched at her grandfather's insidious cleverness. Zach wasn't someone who could be bought, at least not with offers of money or prestige. Instead, Gramps had used a far more subtle form of inducement. He'd addressed Zach's pride, complimented his achievements, flattered him. To hear Gramps tell it, Zachary Thomas was the only man alive capable of taking on the task of becoming Janine's husband.

"What did you tell him?" she asked, her voice so low it was a wonder Zach even heard her.

"No way."

Janine blinked back the surprise that was mingled with a fair amount of indignation. "Just like that? Couldn't you at least have mulled over the decision?" Zach was staring at her as though he thought someone should rush over and take her temperature. "Forget I said that," she muttered, fussing with her napkin in order to avoid meeting his eyes.

"I didn't want to give him any encouragement."

"That was wise." Janine picked up her water glass and downed half the contents.

"To your grandfather's credit, he seemed to accept my answer."

"Don't count on it," Janine warned.

"Don't worry, I know him, too. He isn't going to give up easily. That's the reason I suggested we meet and talk this out. If we keep in touch, we can anticipate Anton's strategy."

"Good idea."

Their salads arrived and Janine frowned when the waitress tossed Zach a suggestive glance. "So," she began in a conversational tone, once the woman had left the table, "Gramps was smart enough not to offer you a large incentive if you went along with his scheme."

"I didn't say that."

She stabbed viciously at her salad. "I hadn't expected him to stoop that low. Exactly what motivational tactics did he use?"

"Not many."

"So it seems," she hissed under her breath.

"He said something about family members having use of the limousine."

Janine's fork made a clanging sound as it hit the side of her salad bowl. "He offered to give you the limousine if you married me? That's all?"

"Not even that," Zach explained, doing a poor job of disguising his amusement, "only the *use* of it."

"Why... why, that's downright insulting." She crammed some salad into her mouth and chewed the crisp lettuce as though it were leather.

"I considered it a step above the cow and ten chickens you suggested the first time we discussed this."

"Fifty-five years ago a cow and ten chickens were worth a lot more than you seem to realize," Janine exclaimed, and immediately regretted raising her voice, because half the patrons in the restaurant turned to stare. She smiled blandly at those around her, then slouched forward over her salad.

She reached for a bread stick, she broke it in half and glared at the dry center. "The use of the limo," she repeated, indignant.

"Don't look so upset. I might have accepted."

Janine knew better. "You weren't even tempted. I assumed Gramps would at least make the offer an appealing one."

Zach was deriving far too much pleasure from this to suit her. "Your attitude isn't helping matters any," she said, frowning righteously.

"I apologize."

But he didn't look the least bit apologetic. When she'd first met Zach, Janine had assumed he was a man who rarely smiled, yet in the short time they'd spent together today, he'd barely been able to keep from laughing outright.

The waitress delivered their clam spaghetti, but when Janine took her first bite, she realized that even the pretense of eating was more than she could manage. She felt too wretched. Tears misted her eyes, which embarrassed her even more, although she struggled to hide the fact that she was upset.

"What's wrong?" Zach surprised her by asking.

Eyes averted, Janine shook her head, while she attempted to swallow. "Gramps believes I'm a poor judge of character." And she was. Brian had proved it to her, but Gramps didn't know anything about Brian. "I feel like a failure."

"He didn't mean any of it," Zach argued gently.

"But couldn't he have come up with something a little more flattering?"

"He needed an excuse to marry you off, otherwise his suggestion would have sounded crazy." Zach hesitated. "Come to think of it, the more we discuss this, the more ludicrous the whole thing seems." He chuckled softly and leaned forward to set his elbows on the table. "Who would ever have believed he'd come up with the idea of the two of us marrying?"

"Thank you very much," Janine muttered. He sat there shredding her ego and apparently found the process just short of hilarious.

"Don't let it get to you. It isn't as if you're interested in me as a husband, anyway."

"You're right about that—you're the last person I'd ever consider marrying," she lashed out, then regretted her reaction when she saw the way his face tightened.

"That's what I thought." He attacked his spaghetti as though the clams were scampering around his plate.

The tension between them mounted. When the waitress arrived to remove their plates, Janine realized she'd barely touched her meal. Zach hadn't eaten much, either.

After paying for their dinner, Zach walked her to her car, offering no further comment. As far as Janine was concerned, their meeting hadn't been the least bit productive. She felt certain that Zach was everything Gramps claimed—incisive, intelligent, intuitive. But that was at the office. As a potential husband and wife, they were completely ill-suited.

"Do you want me to keep in touch?" she asked when she'd unlocked her car door. They stood awkwardly together in the street, and Janine realized they hardly knew what to say to each other.

"I suppose we should, since neither of us is interested in falling in with this plan of his," Zach finally said. "The least we can do is set aside our differences and work together, otherwise we might unknowingly play into his hands."

"I won't be swayed and you won't be, either." Janine found the thought oddly disappointing.

"You don't have anything to worry about on my part," Zach informed her stiffly. "If and when I do marry, which I sincerely doubt, I'll choose my own bride."

It went without saying that Janine was nothing like the woman he'd want to spend his life with.

"If and when I marry, I'll choose my own husband," she said, sounding equally inflexible. As Zach had said not long before, they were as different as satin and burlap.

"I DON'T KNOW if I like boys or not," thirteen-year-old Pam Hudson admitted over a cheeseburger and French fries. "They can be such fools."

It had been a week since Janine's dinner with Zach, and it amazed her that the teenager's assessment of the opposite sex should so closely match her own.

"I'm not even sure I like Charlie anymore," Pam confessed as she stirred her catsup with a French fry. Idly she smeared the red sauce around the edges of the plate in a haphazard pattern. "I used to be so crazy about him, remember?"

Janine smiled indulgently and reminded her. "Every other word was Charlie this and Charlie that."

"He can be okay, though, you know? Remember when he brought me that long-stemmed rose and left it on my porch?"

"I remember." Janine's mind flashed to the first afternoon she'd met Zach. As they left the restaurant together, he'd smiled at her. It wasn't much as smiles went, but for some reason she didn't fully understand, she couldn't seem to forget how he'd held her gaze, his dark eyes gentle, as he murmured polite nonsense. Funny how little things about this man tended to pop up in her mind at the strangest moments.

"But last week," Pam continued, "Charlie was playing basketball with the guys, and when I walked by, he pretended he didn't even know me."

"That smarted, didn't it?"

"You bet it did," Pam confessed. "And after I tie-dyed a shirt for him, too."

"Does he wear it?"

A gratified smile lit the girl's eyes. "All the time."

"By the way, I like how you're combing your hair."

Pam beamed. "I wanted it to look more like yours."

Actually, the style suited Pam far better than it did her, Janine thought. The sides were cut close to the head, but the long bangs flopped with a life of their own, at least on Janine they did. Lately she'd taken to pinning them back.

"How are things at home?" Janine asked, watching the girl carefully. Pam's father, Jerry Hudson, was divorced and had custody of his daughter. Pam's mother worked on the East Coast. With no family in the area, Jerry worried that his daughter needed a woman's influence. He'd contacted the Friendship Club about the same time Janine had applied to be a volunteer. Since Jerry worked odd hours as a short-order cook, she'd met him only once. He was a decent sort, working hard to make a good life for himself and his daughter.

Pam was a marvelous kid, Janine mused, and she possessed exceptional creative talent. Even before her father could afford a sewing machine for her, Pam had been designing and making clothes for her Barbie dolls. The bandanna dress was one of the first projects Pam had completed on her new machine, and she'd proudly presented it to Janine. Pam had made several others since; they were popular with her friends, and she was ecstatic about the success of her ideas.

"I think I might forgive Charlie," the girl went on to say, her look contemplative. "I mean, he was with the guys and everything."

"I suppose it's not cool to let his friends know he's got a girlfriend?"

"Something like that."

Janine wasn't feeling nearly as forgiving toward Zach. He'd made such an issue of their keeping in touch, then hadn't called her once since. She didn't believe for an instant that Gramps had given up on his marriage campaign, but he'd apparently decided to let the matter rest. The pressure was off, yet Janine kept expecting some word from Zach. The least he could do was phone, she grumbled to herself, though she'd made no attempt to analyze the reasons for her disappointment.

"Maybe Charlie isn't so bad, after all," Pam murmured, then added wisely, "This is an awkward age for boys, especially in their relationships with girls."

"Say," Janine teased, "who's supposed to be the adult here, anyway? That's my line."

"Oh, sorry,"

Smiling, Janine stole a French fry from Pam's plate and popped it into her mouth.

"So when are you leaving for Scotland?" Pam wanted to know.

"Next week."

"How long are you going to be gone?"

"Ten days." The trip had come as a complete surprise—a gift from her grandfather. One night shortly after she'd met Zach for dinner, Gramps had handed her an airline ticket. When she'd asked why, his reply had been vague, even cryptic—something about her needing to get away. Since Janine had always dreamed of visiting Scotland, she'd leapt at the offer.

It wasn't until she'd driven Pam home that Janine thought she should let Zach know she was going to be out of the country. It probably wasn't important, but then, he'd made a point of saying they should keep in touch . . .

JANINE PLANNED HER VISIT to the office carefully, making sure Gramps would be occupied elsewhere. Since she'd been shopping for her trip, she was carrying several department and clothing store bags. She was doing this for a reason. She wanted her visit to appear unplanned, as if in the course of a busy day, she'd suddenly remembered their agreement.

"Hello," she said to Zach's efficient secretary, smiling cheerfully. "Is Mr. Thomas available? I'll only need a moment of his time."

The older woman clearly disapproved of this intrusion, but although she pursed her lips, she didn't verbalize her objection. She pushed the intercom button and Janine unexpectedly felt a tingle of awareness at the sound of Zach's strong masculine voice.

"This is a pleasant surprise," he said, standing as Janine breezed into the room with a flair a Paris model might have envied.

She set her bags on the floor and with an exaggerated sigh, eased herself into the chair opposite his desk and crossed her long legs. "I'm sorry to drop in unannounced," she said casually, "but I have some news."

"It's no problem." His gaze fell to the bags heaped on the floor. "Looks like you've had a busy afternoon."

"I was shopping."

"So I see. Any special reason?"

"It's my trousseau." Melodramatically, she pressed the back of her hand against her forehead. "I can't take the pressure anymore. I've come to tell you I've told my grandfather to go ahead and arrange the wedding. Someday, somehow, we'll learn to love each other."

"This charade isn't the least bit amusing. Now what's so important that it can't—"

"Mr. Thomas," his secretary announced crisply over the intercom, "Mr. Hartman is here to see you."

Janine's eyes rounded in panic as her startled gaze flew to Zach, who looked equally alarmed. It would be the worst possible thing for Gramps to discover Janine alone with Zach in his office. She hated to think what interpretation he'd put on that.

"I'll just be a minute," Zach said, reading the hysteria in her eyes. She marveled at how composed he sounded. He pointed toward a closed door and ushered her into a small room—or a huge closet—that was practically a home away from home. A bar, refrigerator, small stove, sink and other conveniences were neatly arranged inside the compact area. No sooner was she inside than the door was slammed shut behind her. The room was in total darkness. A second later, the door was jerked open again, letting in a shaft of light, and three large shopping bags were tossed in.

Janine felt utterly ridiculous. She kept as still as she could, almost afraid to breathe for fear of being discovered.

With her ear pressed against the door, she tried to listen to the conversation, hoping to discover just how long Gramps intended to plant himself in Zach's office.

Unfortunately, she could barely hear a thing. She risked opening the door a crack; a quick glance revealed that both men were turned away from her, presenting her with a clear view of their backs. That explained why she couldn't decipher their conversation.

It was then Janine spotted her purse. Strangling a gasp, she eased the door shut and staggered away from it. She covered her mouth as she took a deep calming breath. When she found the courage to edge open the door and peek again, she saw that all her grandfather had to do was glance downward.

Sweet heaven, if he shuffled his feet, his shoe would catch the strap and he'd drag it out of the office with him.

Zach turned away from the window, and for the first time Janine could hear and see him clearly.

"I'll take care of that right away," he said evenly. He was so calm, so composed, as though he often kept women hidden in his closet. He must have spied Janine's purse because his eyes widened briefly and his gaze flew accusingly toward her.

Well, for heaven's sake, she hadn't purposely left it out there for Gramps to trip over! He wasn't even supposed to be in the building. That very morning, he'd told her he was lunching at the Athletic Club with his longtime friend, Burt Coleman. Whenever Gramps ate the noonday meal with his cronies, he ended up spending the afternoon playing pinochle. Apparently, he'd changed his habits, just so her hair would turn prematurely gray.

Several tortured minutes passed before Zach escorted Gramps to the door. The instant it was closed, Janine stepped into the office, blinking against the brightness after her wait in the dark. "My purse," she said in a strangled voice. "Do you think he saw it?"

"It would be a miracle if he didn't. Of all the stupid things to do."

"I didn't purposely leave it out here!"

"I'm not talking about that," Zach growled. "I'm referring to your coming here in the first place. Are you crazy?"

"I...had something to tell you and I was in the neighborhood." So much for her suave, sophisticated facade. Zach was right, of course; she could have told him just as easily by phone. But for some perverse reason, she'd wanted to tell him in person about her trip.

Zach looked furious. "For the life of me I can't think of a solitary thing that's so important you'd attempt anything this foolish. If your grandfather were to see the two of us together, he'd immediately jump to the wrong conclusion. Until this afternoon, everything's been peaceful. Anton hasn't once mentioned your name and, frankly, I appreciated that."

His words stung. "You're right, of course. I...I won't make the mistake of coming again—ever," she vowed, trying to sound dignified and aloof. She gathered her things as quickly as possible and hurried out of the office, not caring who saw her leave, including Gramps.

"Janine, you never did say why you came." Zach had followed her to the elevator.

Janine stared at the light above the elevator that indicated the floor number, as though it was a message of the utmost importance. Her hold on the bags was precarious, and something was dragging against her feet, but she couldn't have cared less. "I'm sorry to have imposed on your valuable time. Now that I think about it, it wasn't even important."

"Janine," he coaxed, apparently regretting his earlier outburst. "I shouldn't have yelled."

"Yes, I know," she said smoothly. The elevator opened and with as little ceremony as possible, she slipped inside. It wasn't until she was over the threshold that she realized her purse strap was tangled around her feet.

So much for a dignified exit.

CHAPTER FOUR

"THE CASTLE OF CAWDOR was built in the fifteenth century and to this day remains the seat of the earl of Cawdor," the tour guide intoned as Janine and several other sightseers viewed the famous landmark. "William Shakespeare used the castle in his play *Macbeth* for the slaying of King Duncan I, thane of Cawdor, in 1040."

For the first few days of Janine's visit to Scotland, she'd been content to explore on her own. The tours, however, helped fill in the bits and pieces of history she might otherwise have missed.

The castle of Cawdor was in northeastern Scotland. The following day, she planned to rent a car and take a meandering route toward Edinburgh, the political heart of Scotland. From what she'd read, Edinburgh Castle was an ancient fortress, built on a huge rock, that dominated the city's skyline. Gramps had booked reservations for her at an inn on the outskirts of town.

The Bonnie Inn, with its red-tiled roof and black-trimmed gables, had all the charm she'd expected, and more. Janine's room offered more character than comfort, but she felt its welcome as if she were visiting an old friend. A vase filled with fresh flowers and dainty jars of bath salts awaited her.

Eager to explore, she strolled outside and investigated the extensive garden. There was a chill in the April air and she tucked her hands in her pockets, watching with amusement as the partridges fed on the lush green lawn.

"Janine?"

At the sound of her name, she turned, and to her astonishment discovered Zach standing not more than ten feet away. "What are you doing here?" she demanded.

"Me? I was about to ask you the same question."

"I'm on vacation. Gramps gave me the trip as a gift."

"I'm here on business," Zach explained, and his brow tightened into a suspicious frown.

Janine was doing her own share of frowning. "This is all rather convenient, don't you think?"

Zach took immediate offense. "You don't honestly believe I planned this, do you?"

"No," she agreed reluctantly.

Zach continued to stand there, stiff and wary. "I had absolutely nothing to do with this," he stated.

"If you hadn't been so rude to me the last time we met," she felt obliged to inform him, with a righteous tilt to her chin, "you'd have known well in advance that Gramps was sending me here, and we could have avoided this unpleasant surprise."

"If you hadn't been in such an all-fired hurry to leave my office, you'd have discovered I was traveling here myself."

"Oh, that's perfect! Go ahead and blame me for everything," she shrieked, glowering at him. "As I recall you were madder than a wet hen at my being anywhere near your precious office."

"All right, I'll admit I might have handled the situation poorly," Zach said, and the muscles in his jaw hardened. "But as you'll recall, I did apologize."

"Sure you did," she said, "after you'd trampled all over my ego. I've never felt more of a fool in my life."

"You?" Zach shouted. "It may surprise you to know I don't make a habit of hiding women in my office."

"Do you think I enjoyed being stuffed in that . . . closet like a bag of dirty laundry?"

"What was I supposed to do? Hide you under my desk?"

"It might have been better than a pitch-black closet."

"If you're so keen on casting blame, let me remind you, I wasn't the one who left my purse in full view of your grandfather," Zach said. "I did everything but perform card tricks to draw his attention away from it."

"You make the entire episode sound like I'm the one at fault," Janine snapped.

"I'm not the one who popped in unexpectedly. If you had a job like everyone else . . ."

"If I had a job," she echoed, outraged. "You mean all the volunteer work I do doesn't count? Apparently the thirty hours a week I put in mean nothing. Sure I've got a degree. Sure I could probably have my pick of a dozen different jobs, but why take employment away from someone who really needs it when so many worthwhile organizations are hurting for volunteers?" She was breathless by the time she finished, and so angry she could feel the heat radiating from her face.

She refused to tolerate Zach's offensive insinuations any longer. From the first time they'd met, Zach had clearly viewed her as spoiled and frivolous, without a brain in her head. And it seemed that nothing had altered his opinion.

"Listen, I didn't mean—"

"It's obvious to me," she cut in bluntly, "that you and I are never going to agree on anything." She was so furious she could barely keep her anger in check. "The best thing for us to do is completely ignore one another. It is quite apparent that you don't want anything to do with me and, frankly, I feel the same way about you. So, good day, Mr. Thomas." With that she walked away, her head high and her pride intact.

For the very first time with this man, she'd been able to make a grand exit. It should have felt good. But it didn't.

An hour later, after Janine had taken the tourist bus into Edinburgh, she found she was still brooding over her latest encounter with Zachary Thomas. If there was any humor at all in this situation, it had to be the fact that her usually sage grandfather could possibly believe she and Zach were in any way suited to each other.

Determined to put the man out of her mind, Janine wandered down Princes Street, which was packed with shoppers, troupes of actors giving impromptu performances, and strolling musicians. Her mood couldn't help but be influenced by the festive flavor, and she soon found herself smiling despite the unpleasant confrontation with her grandfather's business partner.

Several of the men who passed her in the street were dressed in kilts and traditional woolen caps called

Glengarries. Janine felt as if she'd stepped into another time, another world, as the air swirled with bagpipe music. The city itself seemed gray and gloomy, a dull background for the colorful sights and sounds, the excitement, of ages past.

It was as Janine walked out of a dress shop that she bumped into Zach a second time. He stopped, his eyes registering surprise and what looked to Janine like a hint of regret—as though confronting her twice in the same day was enough to try anyone's patience.

"I know what you're thinking," he said, pinning her with his dark intense gaze.

"And I'm equally confident that you don't." She gathered her packages close and edged against the shop window to avoid hindering other pedestrians on the crowded sidewalk.

"I came here to do some shopping," Zach said gruffly. "I wasn't following you."

"You can rest assured I wasn't traipsing after *you*."

"Fine," he said.

"Fine," she repeated.

But neither of them moved for several nerve-racking seconds. Janine assumed Zach was going to say something else. Perhaps she secretly hoped he would. If it was impossible for them to be friends, Janine would have preferred that they remain allies. They should be uniting their forces instead of battling each other. Without a word, Zach gestured abruptly and wheeled around to join the stream of people hurrying down the sidewalk.

A half hour later, with more packages added to her collection, Janine strolled into a fabric store, wanting to purchase a sizable length of wool as a gift for Pam. She ran her fingertips along several thick bolts of material, marveling at the bold color combinations. The wool felt soft, but when she lifted a corner with her palm, she was amazed at how heavy it was.

"Each clan has its own tartan," the white-haired lady in the shop explained. Janine enjoyed listening to her voice, with its enthusiastic warmth and distinct Scottish burr. "Some of the best-known tartans come in three patterns that are to be worn for different occasions—everyday, dress and battle."

Intrigued, Janine watched as the congenial woman walked around the table to remove a blue-and-green plaid. Janine had already seen that pattern several times. The shop owner continued by explaining that tourists were often interested in this particular tartan, called Black Watch, because it was assigned to no particular clan. In choosing Black Watch, they weren't aligning themselves with any one clan, but showing total impartiality.

Pleased, Janine purchased several yards of the fabric. She was shuffling her packages in her arms as she made her way down the narrow street when she caught sight of Zach watching a troupe of musicians. She started to move away, then for no reason she could name, paused to study him. Her view of him really hadn't changed since that first afternoon. She still thought Zach Thomas opinionated, unreasonable, and...all right, she was willing to admit it, attractive. *Very* attractive, in a sort of rough-hewn way. He lacked the polish, the superficial sophistication of a man like Brian, but he had a vigor that seemed thoroughly masculine. He also had the uncanny ability to set her teeth on edge with a single look. No other man could irritate her so quickly.

The musicians began a lively song and Zach laughed unself-consciously. His rich husky tenor sounded smooth and relaxed as it drifted across the street toward her. Janine knew she should have pulled away then, but she couldn't. Despite everything, she was intrigued.

Zach must have felt her scrutiny because he suddenly turned and their eyes locked before Janine could withdraw her gaze. The color rose to her cheeks and for a long moment, neither moved. Neither smiled.

It was in Janine's mind to cross the street, swallow her pride, and put an end to this pointless antagonism. In the past several weeks her pride had become familiar fare; serving it up once more shouldn't be all that difficult.

She was entertaining that thought when a bus drove past her belching a thick cloud of black smoke, momentarily blocking her view of Zach. When the bus had passed, Janine noticed he'd returned his attention to the musicians.

Disheartened, she headed in the opposite direction. She hadn't gone more than a block when she heard him call her name.

She stopped and waited for him to join her. With an inquiring lift of an eyebrow, he reached for some of her packages. She nodded, repressing a shiver of excitement as his hand brushed hers. Shifting his burden, he slowed his steps to match Janine's. Then he spoke for the first time. "We need to talk."

"I don't see how we can. Every time you open your mouth you say something insulting and offensive."

Only moments earlier, Janine had been hoping to put an end to this foolishness, yet here she was provoking an argument, acting just as unreasonable as she accused him of being. She stopped midstep, disgusted with herself. "I shouldn't have said that. I don't know what it is about us, but we seem to have a difficult time being civil to each other."

"It might have something to do with the shock of finding one another here."

"Which brings up another subject," Janine added fervently. "If Gramps was going to arrange for us to meet, why send us both halfway around the world to do it?"

"I used to think I knew your grandfather," Zach murmured. "But lately, I'm beginning to wonder. I haven't a clue why he chose Scotland."

"He came to me with the airline ticket, reminding me it'd been almost a year since I'd traveled anywhere," Janine said. "He told me it was high time I took a vacation, that I needed to get away for a while. And I bought it hook, line and sinker."

"You?" Zach cried, shaking his head, clearly troubled. "Your grandfather sent me here on a wild-goose chase. Yes, there were contacts to make, but this was a trip any one of our junior executives could have handled. It wasn't until I arrived at the inn and found you booked there that I realized what he was up to."

"If we hadn't been so caught up with who was to blame for that fiasco at your office, we might have been able to prevent this. At least, we'd have realized what Gramps was doing."

"Exactly," Zach said. "Forewarned is forearmed. Obviously, we've got to put aside our differences and stay in communication. That's the key. Communication."

"Absolutely," Janine agreed, with a firm nod of her head.

"But finding ourselves thrown together at every opportunity is only going to lead to trouble."

"I couldn't agree with you more."

"The less time we spend together, the better." He paused when he noticed she was standing in front of the bus stop.

"If we allow Gramps to throw us together like this, it'll only encourage him. We've got to be very firm about this, before things get completely out of hand."

"You're right." Without asking, he took the rest of the packages from her arms, adding them to the bags and parcels he already carried. "I rented a car. I don't suppose you'd accept a ride back to the inn?"

"Please." Janine was grateful for the offer. They'd started off badly, each willing to blame the other, but fortunately their relationship was beginning to improve. That pleased her. She'd much rather have Zachary for a friend than an enemy.

They spoke very little on the twenty-mile ride back to the Bonnie Inn. After an initial exchange of what sites they'd viewed and what they'd purchased, there didn't seem to be much more to say. They remained awkward and a little uneasy with each other. Battle-weary. And Janine was all too aware of how intimate the confines of the small rented car were. Her shoulder and her thigh were within scant inches of brushing against Zach, something she was determined to ignore.

The one time Janine chanced a look in his direction, she noticed how intent his features were, as if he were driving a difficult and dangerous course instead of a well-maintained road with only light traffic. His mouth was compressed, bracketed by deep grooves, and his dark eyes had narrowed. He glanced away from the road long enough for their eyes to meet. Janine smiled and quickly looked away, embarrassed that he'd caught her studying him so closely. She wished she could sort through her feelings, analyze all her contradictory emotions in a logical manner. She was attracted to Zach, but not in the same way she'd been attracted to Brian. Although Zach infuriated her, she admired him. Respected him. But he didn't send her senses whirling mindlessly, as Brian had. Then again, she didn't think of him as a brother, either. Her only conclusion was that her feelings for Zach were more confusing than ever.

After thanking him for the ride and collecting her parcels, she left Zach in the lobby and tiredly climbed the stairs to her room. She soaked in a hot scented bath, then changed into a blue-and-gold plaid kilt she'd bought that afternoon. With it, she wore a thin white sweater under her navy-blue blazer. She tied a navy scarf at her neck, pleased with the effect. A little blush, a dab of eye shadow and she was finished, by now more than ready for something to eat.

Zach was waiting to be seated in the dining room when she came downstairs. He wore a thick hand-knit sweater over black dress slacks and made such a virile sight she found it difficult not to stare.

The hostess greeted them both with a warm smile. "Dinner for two?"

Janine reacted first, flustered and a little embarrassed. "We're not together," she said quickly. "This gentleman was here before me." Anything else would be negating the agreement they'd made earlier.

Zach frowned as he followed the hostess to a table set against the wall, close to the massive stone fireplace. The hostess returned and directed Janine to a table against the same wall, so close to Zach that she could practically read the menu over his shoulder. She was reading her own menu when Zach spoke. "Don't you think we're both being a little silly?"

"Yes," she admitted. "But we agreed this afternoon that being thrown together like this could lead to trouble."

"I honestly don't think it would hurt either of us to have dinner together, do you?"

"No...I don't think it would." They'd spend the entire meal talking across the tables to each other, anyway.

He stood up, grinning. "May I join you?"

"Please." She couldn't help responding with a smile.

He pulled out the chair across from her, his gaze appreciative. "Those colors look good on you."

"Thanks." She had to admit he looked darkly vibrant—and wonderfully masculine—himself. She was about to return his compliment when it dawned on her how senselessly they were challenging fate.

"It's happening already," she whispered heatedly, leaning toward him in order not to be overheard.

"What?" Zach glanced around him as though he expected ghostly clansmen to emerge from behind the thick drapes.

"You're telling me how good I look in blue and I was about to tell you how nice you look and we're smiling at each other and forming a mutual admiration society. Before either of us will be able to figure out what happened, we'll be married."

"That's ridiculous."

"Sure, you say that now, but I can see real trouble here."

"Does this mean you want me to go back to my table and eat alone?"

"Of course not. I just think it would be best if we limited the compliments. All right?"

"I'll never say anything nice about you again."

Satisfied, Janine nodded. "Thank you."

"You might want to watch that, as well," he warned with a roguish grin. "If we're too formal and polite with each other, that could lead us straight to the jewelers. Before we know what's happening, we'll be choosing wedding bands."

Janine's lips quivered with a barely restrained smile. "I hadn't thought about that." They glanced at each other and before either could hold it in, they were laughing, attracting the attention of everyone in the dining room. As abruptly as they'd started, they stopped, burying their faces in the menus.

After they'd ordered, Janine shared her theory with Zach, a theory that had come to her on their drive back to the inn. "I think I know why Gramps arranged for us to meet here."

"I'm dying to hear this."

"Actually, I'm afraid I'm the one responsible." She slumped against the shield-back chair and heaved a sigh of remorse. Every part of her seemed aware of Zach, which was exactly what she didn't want. She sighed again. "When Gramps first mentioned the idea of an arranged marriage, I tried to make him understand that love wasn't something one ordered like...like dinner from a menu. He genuinely didn't seem to grasp what I was saying and wanted to know what a woman needed to fall in love."

"And you told him a trip to Scotland?" Zach's eyes sparkled with the question.

"Of course not. I told him a woman needed romance."

Zach leaned forward. "I hate to appear dense, but I seem to have missed something."

Pretending to be annoyed with him, Janine explained, "Well, Gramps asked me to define romance..."

"I'd be interested in finding that out myself." Zach wiped the edges of his mouth with his napkin. Janine suspected he did it to cover a growing need to smile.

"It isn't all that easy to explain, you know," Janine said. "And remember this was off the top of my head. I told Gramps romance was forbidden trysts on Scottish moors."

"With an enemy clan chieftain?"

"No, with the man I loved."

"What else did you tell him?"

"I don't remember exactly. As I recall, I said something about a moonlight stroll on the beach, and desperate passion."

"I wonder how he'll arrange that?"

"I don't think I want to find out," Janine murmured. In light of how seriously Gramps had taken her impromptu definition, she almost dreaded the thought of what he might do next.

When they'd finished, their plates were removed by the attentive waiter and their coffee served. To complicate her feelings, she found she was a little sad their dinner was about to end.

They left the dining room, and Zach escorted her up the stairs. "Thank you for being willing to take a risk and share dinner with me," he said, his voice deadpan. "I enjoyed it, despite the, uh, danger."

"I did, too," Janine said softly. More than she cared to admit. Against her better judgment, her mind spun with possible ways to delay their parting, but she decided against each one, not wanting to tempt fate any more than she already had.

Zach walked her to her room, pausing outside her door. Janine found herself searching for the right words. She longed to tell him that she'd enjoyed spending the evening with him, talking and laughing together, but she didn't know how to say it without sounding like a woman in love.

Zach appeared to be having the same problem. He raised one hand as though to touch her face, then apparently changed his mind, dropping his hand abruptly. She felt strangely disappointed.

"Good night," he said curtly, stepping back.

"Good night," she echoed, turning to walk into her room. She closed the door and leaned against it, feeling unsettled but at a loss to understand why.

After ten restless minutes she ventured out again. The country garden was well lit, and a paved pathway led to rocky cliffs that fell off sharply. Even from where she stood, Janine could hear the sea roaring below. She could smell its salty tang, mixed with the scent of heath, a wild purple flower that bloomed in spring. Thrusting her hands into her blazer pockets, Janine strolled along a narrow path into the garden. The night air was cool and she had no intention of walking far, not more than a few hundred feet. She'd return in the morning when there was much more to be seen. Then she planned to walk as far as the cliffs with their buffeting winds.

The moon was full and so large it seemed to take up the entire sky, sending streaks of silvery light across the horizon. With her arms cradling her middle, she gazed up at it, certain she'd never felt more peaceful or serene. She closed her eyes, savoring the luxurious silence of the moment.

Suddenly it was broken. "So we meet again," Zach said from behind her.

"This is getting ridiculous." Janine turned to him and smiled, her heart beating hard and fast. "Meeting on the moors..."

"It isn't exactly a tryst," Zach said.

"Not technically."

They stood side by side, looking into the night sky, both at a loss for words. During their meal they'd talked nonstop, but now Janine felt tongue-tied and ill at ease. If they'd been worried about having dinner together, they were placing themselves at even greater risk alone in the moonlight.

Janine knew it. Zach knew it. But neither suggested leaving.

"It's a beautiful night," Zach said at last, linking his hands behind his back.

"It is, isn't it?" Janine replied brightly, as if he'd introduced the most stimulating topic of her entire vacation.

"I don't think we should put any stock in this," he surprised her by saying next.

"In what?"

"In meeting here, as if we'd arranged a tryst. Of course you're a beautiful woman and it would only be natural if a man... any red-blooded man were to find himself charmed. I'd blame it on the moonlight, wouldn't you?"

"Oh, I agree completely. I mean, we've been thrust together and it would only be natural if the two of

us . . . were to find ourselves momentarily . . . attracted
to each other. That would be normal, but it doesn't
mean anything.''

Zach moved behind her. ''You're right, of course.''
He hesitated, then murmured, ''You should have worn
a thicker jacket.'' Before she could assure him she was
perfectly comfortable, he ran his hands slowly down
the length of her arms, as though to warm her. Unable to restrain herself, Janine sighed softly and leaned
against him, soaking up his warmth and his strength.

''This presents something of a problem, doesn't it?''
he whispered, his voice husky and close to her ear.
''Isn't moonlight supposed to do something strange to
people?''

''I . . . think it only affects werewolves.''

He chuckled and his breath shot a series of incredible light-as-air sensations along her neck. Janine felt
she was about to crumple at his feet. Then his chin
brushed the side of her face and she sighed once more,
delighting in the baffling exciting feel of him.

His hands on her shoulders, Zach urged her around
so that she faced him, but not for anything would Janine allow her gaze to meet his.

He didn't say anything.

She didn't, either.

Janine suffered a series of mixed worries, afraid to
voice even one. Zach apparently felt the same way,
because he didn't seem any more eager to explain
things than she did. Or to stop them. . . .

After a moment, Zach pressed his hands over her
cheekbones. Leisurely, his thumbs stroked the line of
her jaw, her chin. His eyes were dark, his expression
unreadable. Janine's heart was churning over and

over, dragging her emotions with it. She swallowed tightly, then moistened her lips.

He seemed to find her mouth mesmerizing, and focused his gaze there. From somewhere deep inside her, she found the strength to warn him that her grandfather's plan was working. She opened her mouth to speak, but before she could utter a single word, Zach's arms came around her and drew her close against his strongly muscled body. She felt his comforting warmth seep through her, smelled the faint muskiness of his skin. The sensations were unlike anything she'd ever experienced. Then he lowered his mouth to hers.

The immediate shock of pleasure the contact sent through her was almost frightening. She couldn't keep from trembling.

He drew back slightly. "You're cold. You should have said something."

"No, that's not it." Even her voice was quivering.

"Then what is?"

In response she kissed him back. She hadn't meant to, but before she could stop herself, she wove her arms around his neck and slanted her mouth over his. She was immersing herself in his strength, just as he was immersing himself in her tenderness.

Zach's shoulders were heaving when at last she pulled her mouth away and pressed her face against his chest.

"Dear Lord," he whispered. He hastily broke away from her as if he'd suddenly realized what they were doing.

Janine was too stunned to react. In an effort to hide his effect on her, she rubbed her hands over her face as though struggling to wake up from a deep sleep.

"That shouldn't have happened," Zach said stiffly.

"You're telling me," she returned raggedly. "It certainly wasn't the smartest move we could have made."

Zach jerked his fingers roughly through his hair and frowned. "I don't know what came over me. Over us. We both know better."

"It probably has something to do with the moon and the fact that we're both tired," Janine said soothingly, offering a convenient excuse. "When you stop to think about it, the whole thing's perfectly understandable. Gramps arranged this meeting, hoping something like this would happen. Clearly the power of suggestion is stronger than either of us realized."

"Clearly." But he continued to frown.

"Oh, gee," Janine said glancing at her watch, unable to read the numbers in the dark. Her voice was high and wavering. "Will you look at the time? I can't believe it's so late. I really should be getting back inside."

"Janine, listen. I think we should talk about this."

"Sure, but not now." All she wanted to do was escape and gather some perspective on what had happened. It had all started so innocently, almost a game, but quickly turned into something far more serious.

"All right, we'll discuss it in the morning." Zach didn't sound too pleased. He walked through the garden with her, muttering under his breath. "Damn it!" he roared, again shoving his fingers through his hair. "Damn it, I knew I should never have come out here."

"There's no need to be so angry. Blame this crisp clean air. It obviously disrupts the brain and interferes with the wave patterns or something."

"Right," Zach said, his voice still gruff.

"Well, good night," Janine managed cheerfully when they reached the staircase.

"Good night," Zach returned, his tone equally nonchalant.

Once Janine was in her room, she threw herself on the bed and covered her eyes with one hand. Oh, no, she lamented silently. They'd crossed the line. Tempted fate. Spit in the eye of common sense.

They'd kissed.

Several minutes later, still shaking, Janine got up and undressed. She slid under the blankets and tried to find a relaxing position. But she didn't feel the least bit like sleeping. Tomorrow she'd have to make polite conversation with Zach and she didn't know if she could bear it. She was sure he'd feel just as uncomfortable with her. She'd noted how he could barely look at her when they entered the inn.

Tossing aside the blankets, Janine decided there was only one option left. She had to leave Scotland, and the sooner the better. Reaching for the phone, she called the airport, booked a seat on the earliest flight home and immediately set about packing her bags.

Not bothering to even try to sleep, she crept down the stairs a little before midnight and checked out of the inn.

"You're leaving sooner than you anticipated, aren't you, Miss Hartman?" the night manager asked, after calling for a cab.

"Yes," she said.

"I hope everything was satisfactory?"

"It was wonderful." She pulled a folded piece of paper from her purse and placed it on the counter. "Would you see to it that Mr. Thomas receives this in the morning?"

"Of course." The young man tucked it in a small cubbyhole behind him.

Satisfied that Zach would know she was leaving and wouldn't be concerned by her hurried return to Seattle, she turned away from the desk and sat in a chair in the small lobby to wait for the cab.

About fifteen minutes later, Janine watched silently as the cabdriver stowed her luggage in the trunk. She paused before climbing into the back seat of the car and glanced one last time at the muted moonlit landscape, disappointed that she wouldn't have an opportunity to visit the cliffs.

The ride to the airport seemed to take an eternity. She felt a burning sense of regret at leaving Scotland. She'd fallen in love with the country during her short visit and hoped someday to return. Although the memory of her evening stroll through the garden would always bring with it a certain chagrin, she couldn't completely regret that time with Zach. In fact, she would always remember the contentment she'd experienced in his arms. She wasn't foolish enough to give it any credence, however.

Janine arrived at the airport several hours before her flight was scheduled to leave. She spent the time drinking coffee and glancing through fashion magazines, several of which she tucked in her luggage to give to Pam later.

Carrying a cup of coffee in one hand, she approached the airline counter with her ticket in the other. By accident, the bag she had draped over her shoulder collided with the man standing next to her.

An automatic apology formed on her lips, but before she could voice it, that same man turned to face her.

"Zach," she cried, nearly dropping her coffee in shock. "What are you doing here?"

CHAPTER FIVE

"YOU THINK this is intentional, don't you?" Zach demanded. "It's obvious you're the one traipsing after me this time. You found the note I slipped under your door and—"

"I checked out just before midnight so I couldn't possibly have read your note," she returned stiffly. She noticed that he didn't mention the message she'd left for him at the front desk. "And furthermore I left word for you."

"I didn't get it."

"Then there's been a misunderstanding."

"To say the least," Zach muttered. "A misunderstanding..." His tone was doubtful, as if he suspected she'd purposely arranged to fly home with him. A sense of righteous indignation filled her, and she launched into a heated protest.

"Excuse me, please."

The interruption was from a uniformed airline employee who was leaning over the counter and waving in an effort to gain their attention.

"May I have your ticket?" she asked Janine. "You're holding up the line."

"Of course. I'm sorry." The best thing to do, she decided, was to ignore Zach completely. Just because they were booked on the same flight home didn't mean they had to have anything to do with each other. Evidently they'd both panicked after their encounter in the garden. He was as eager to escape as she was.

Okay, so she'd ignore him and he'd ignore her. She'd return to her life, and he'd return to his. From this point forward, they need never have contact with each other again. Then they'd both be satisfied.

The clerk took the ticket from Janine and punched several numbers into her computer. "I'll give you your seat assignment now," she remarked, concentrating on the screen.

Standing on tiptoe, Janine leaned toward the woman and lowered her voice to a whisper. "Could you make sure I'm as far removed from Mr. Thomas's seat as possible?"

"Miss," the attendant said impatiently, "this flight is booked solid and has for weeks. The only reason we were able to give you and your . . . friend seats was because of a last-minute cancellation. I'll do the best I can, but I can't rearrange everyone's seat assignments just before the flight."

"I understand," Janine said, feeling foolish and petty. But the way her luck had been running, Zach would end up sitting in the seat beside her, believing she'd purposely arranged that, too.

They boarded the flight separately; in fact, Zach was one of the last passengers to step onto the plane.

By that time, Janine was settled in the second row of the first-class section, flipping through the pages of the flight magazine. Zach strolled past her, intent on the ticket clenched tightly in his hand.

Pretending she hadn't seen him seemed the best tactic, and she turned to gaze out the window.

"It seems I've been assigned to sit here," Zach announced brusquely, loading his carry-on luggage in the compartment above the seats.

Janine had to bite her tongue to keep from insisting she'd had nothing to do with that. She'd even tried to prevent it, but she doubted Zach would have believed her.

"Before you claim otherwise, I want you to know I didn't arrange this," he said, sitting down stiffly beside her.

"I know that."

"You do?"

"Of course," Janine confirmed. "The fates are against us. I don't know how my grandfather arranged our meeting at the airport or the adjoining seats, any more than I know why I stumbled on you my first day at the Bonnie Inn. We might never have crossed paths. But somehow, some way, Gramps is responsible." She thought it best not to mention their stroll in the moonlight. If it was important to lay blame for that, she'd accept it.

"So you're not ready to unleash the full force of your anger on me?"

"I don't see how I can be upset with you—or the reverse. Neither of us asked for this."

"Exactly."

Janine yawned loudly and covered her mouth. "Oh, excuse me. I didn't sleep last night and now it's catching up with me."

Her yawn was contagous and soon Zach's hand was warding off his own admission of drowsiness. The flight attendant came by with coffee, which both Zach and Janine declined.

"Frankly, I'd be more interested in a pillow," Janine said yawning again. The attendant handed her one, a thick blanket and a couple of small pillows, then offered the same to Zach. He refused both, intending to work on some papers he'd withdrawn from his briefcase. The minute the plane was safely in the air, Janine laid her head back and closed her eyes. Almost immediately she felt herself drifting into a peaceful slumber.

She stirred twice in the long hours that followed, but both times a gentle voice soothed her back to sleep. Sighing, she snuggled into the warmth, feeling more comfortable than she had in weeks.

She began to dream and could see herself walking across the moors, wearing traditional Scottish dress, while bagpipes wailed in the background.

Then, on the crest of a hill, Zach appeared, lavishly dressed in a Black Watch kilt and tam-o'-shanter; a set of bagpipes was draped over his shoulder. Their eyes met and the music ceased. Then out of nowhere her grandfather appeared, standing halfway between the two of them, looking pleased and excited. He cupped his hands over his mouth and shouted to Janine.

"Is this romance?"

"Yes," she shouted back.

"What else do you need?"

"Love."

"Love," Gramps repeated, frowning. He turned to Zach, apparently seeking some kind of assistance.

Zach started fiddling with the bagpipes, avoiding the question. He scowled as he concentrated on his task.

"Look at the pair of you," Gramps called. "You're perfect together. Zach, when are you going to wake up and realize what a beauty my Janine is?"

"If I do marry, you can be sure I'll choose my own bride." Zach hollered.

"You!" Janine shouted back. "I'd prefer to pick out my own husband!"

"You're falling in love with Zach!" Gramps declared, elated.

"I—I—" Janine was so flustered she couldn't complete her thought, which only served to please her grandfather more.

"Look at her, boy," Gramps directed his attention back to Zach. "See how lovely she is. And think of what beautiful children you'll have."

"Gramps! Enough about our beautiful babies! I'm not marrying Zach!"

"Janine." Zach's voice echoed in her ear.

"Keep out of this," she cried. He was the last person she wanted to hear from.

"You're having a dream."

Her eyes fluttered open to discover Zach's face unbelievably close to her own and her head nestled against his chest. "Oh..." she mumbled, bolting upright. "Oh, dear...I am sorry. I didn't realize I was leaning on you."

"I hated to wake you, but you seemed to be having a nightmare."

She blinked against the lights and tried to focus her attention on him, but it was difficult, and to complicate matters her eyes started to water. She wiped her face with one sleeve, then straightening, she removed the pillows from behind her back and folded the blanket, doing her best to disguise how badly her hands were trembling.

"You're worried about what happened after dinner last night, aren't you?"

Janine released a pent-up breath, and smiled at him brightly as she lied. "Nothing really happened."

"In the garden, when we kissed. Listen," Zach said in a low voice, glancing quickly around to ensure that no one could overhear their conversation, "I think it's time we talked this out."

"I... You're right, of course." She didn't feel up to this, but she supposed it was best dealt with before she had to face her grandfather.

"Egos aside."

"By all means," Janine agreed. She braced herself, not knowing what to expect. Zach had made his views on the idea of an arranged marriage plain from the first; for that matter so had she. Brian had taught her a valuable lesson, a painful lesson, one that wouldn't easily be forgotten. She'd given him her heart and her trust, and he'd betrayed both. Falling in love had been the most shattering experience of her life, and she had no intention of repeating it any time soon.

"I'd be a liar if I didn't admit how pleasant kissing you was," Zach said, "but I wish it had never happened. It created more problems than it solved."

Janine wasn't exactly flattered by his admission. Keeping egos out of this was harder than it sounded, she thought ruefully. Her face must have spelled out her thoughts because Zach elaborated. "Before I arrived in Scotland, we barely knew each other. We met that first afternoon over lunch—with Anton—and talked a couple of times, but basically we remained strangers."

"We had dinner one night," Janine reminded him, irked he could so casually dismiss that evening.

"Right," he acknowledged. "Then we met at the Bonnie Inn and, bingo, we were having dinner together and strolling in the moonlight, and before either of us quite knew how it happened, we were kissing."

Janine nodded, listening quietly.

"There are several factors we can take into account, but if we were going to place blame for that kiss, I'm afraid I'm the one at fault."

"You?"

"Me," he confirmed with a grimace. "Actually, I'm prepared to accept full responsibility. I doubt you were aware of what was happening. It didn't take me long to realize you're completely innocent—"

"Now just a minute," Janine snapped. Once more he was taking potshots at her dignity. "What do you mean by that?"

"It's obvious you haven't had a lot of sexual experience and—"

"In other words I'm so incredibly naive that I couldn't possibly be held accountable for a few kisses in the moonlight?"

"Something like that."

"Oh, brother," she muttered.

"There's no need to feel offended."

"I wasn't exactly raised in a convent school, you know. And for your information, I've been kissed by more than one man."

"I'm sure you have. We're getting sidetracked here—"

"I'm sorry you found me so inept. A man of your vast worldly experience must have been sorely disappointed by someone as unsophisticated and artless as me, and—"

"Janine," he said firmly, stopping her. "You're putting words in my mouth. All I was saying is that we—*I*—let matters get out of hand and we can't blame your grandfather for what happened."

"I'm willing to accept my part in this. I can also see where this conversation is leading."

"Good," Zach said. It was clear his composure was slipping. "You tell me."

"You think that because I enjoyed spending time with you and we shared this mildly romantic evening and—"

"Mildly romantic?"

"Yes, you did say egos aside, didn't you? I'm just being honest."

"Fine," he said, tight-lipped.

"Now you seem to think that because you have so much more experience than I do, there's a real danger I'd swoon at your feet if we repeated the experience." She rested her hand over her heart in melodramatic fashion and batted her eyelashes furiously.

"Janine, you're behaving like a child," he informed her coldly.

"Of course I am. That's exactly what you seem to expect of me."

Zach's fingers tightened on the armrest. "You're purposely misconstruing everything I said."

"Frankly, whatever you're trying to say isn't necessary. You're thinking that we had a borderline interest in each other and now we've crossed that border. Right? Well, I'm telling you that you needn't concern yourself." She sucked in a deep breath and glared at him. "I'm right, aren't I? That's what you think, isn't it?"

"Something like that, yes."

Janine nodded grimly. "And now you think because you've held me in your arms and you lost your control long enough to kiss me, I'm suddenly going to start entertaining thoughts of the M word."

"The M word?"

"Marriage."

"That's ridiculous," Zach said, forcefully returning the flight magazine to the seat pocket in front of him.

"Well?" she demanded.

"I think the temptation might be there and we should both beware of that type of thought."

"Oh, honestly, Zach," she said sarcastically, "you overestimate yourself."

"Listen, I wasn't the one mumbling something about our having beautiful babies. We kiss, and the next thing I know you're studying diaper-folding techniques."

"I was having a dream! That has absolutely nothing to do with what we're talking about now."

"You could've fooled me." He reached for the same magazine he'd recently rejected and turned the pages hard enough to rip them in two. "I don't think this discussion is getting us anywhere."

Janine sighed. "You were right, though. We did need to clear the air."

Zach made a gruff indistinguishable reply.

"I promise to do my best to keep out of your magnetic force field, but if I occasionally succumb to your overwhelming charm and forget myself, I can only beg your forgiveness."

"Enough, Janine."

He looked so annoyed with her that she couldn't help smiling. Zach Thomas was a man of such colossal ego it would serve him right if she pretended to faint every time he glanced in her direction. The image filled her mind with laughter.

Zach leaned his head back and closed his eyes, effectively concluding their conversation. Janine gazed out the window at the first signs of sunrise, thinking about all kinds of things—except her chaotic feelings for the man beside her.

After what seemed a lifetime, the pilot announced that the plane would soon be approaching Seattle-Tacoma International Airport. Home sounded good to Janine, although she fully intended to have a heart-to-heart talk with her grandfather about his matchmaking efforts.

Once they'd landed, she cleared customs quickly. She struggled with her two large pieces of luggage, pulling one by the handle and looping the long strap of the second over her shoulder. Zach was still dealing with the customs agent when she maneuvered her way outside into the bright morning sunlight, intending to flag down a cab.

"Here," Zach said, joining her, "I'll carry one of those for you." He'd managed to travel with only his briefcase and one garment bag, which was neatly folded and easily handled.

"Thank you," she said breathlessly.

"I thought we'd agreed to limit our expressions of gratitude toward each other," he grumbled, frowning as he lifted the suitcase.

"I apologize. It slipped my mind."

Zach continued to grumble. "What'd you pack in here, anyway? Bricks?"

"If you're going to complain, I'll carry it myself."

He muttered something she couldn't hear and shook his head. "I'll get us a cab."

"Us?"

"We're going to confront your grandfather."

"Together? Now?" She was exhausted, mentally and physically. They both were.

"The sooner the better, don't you think?"

The problem was, Janine hadn't given much thought to what she was going to say. She fully intended to challenge Gramps but she'd planned to wait for the most opportune time. And she'd hoped to speak to him privately. "He might not even be home," she argued, "and if he is, I don't know if now would really be best."

"I want this matter settled once and for all."

"So do I," she said vehemently. "But I think we should choose when and how we do this a little more carefully, don't you?"

"Perhaps…" His agreement seemed hesitant, even grudging. "All right, we'll do it your way."

"It isn't my way. It just makes sense to organize our thoughts first. Trust me, Zach, I want this thing cleared up as badly as you do."

His reply was little more than a grunt, but whether it was a comment on the weight of her suitcase or her tactics in dealing with Anton, she didn't know.

"And furthermore," she said, making a sweeping motion with her arm, "we've got to stop doubting each other. Nobody's following anyone and neither of us is in any danger of falling in love because we were foolish enough to kiss."

"Fine," Zach muttered as he set her suitcase down. He raised his hand to hail a taxi. To Janine's mingled relief and annoyance, a cab immediately squealed to a halt by the curb.

"How is it we always seem to agree with each other and yet we constantly find ourselves at odds?"

"I wish I knew," he said, looking weary in body and spirit. The cabdriver jumped out and opened the trunk, storing her suitcases neatly inside. Zach threw his garment bag in on top.

"We might as well still share this taxi," he said, holding the door for her.

"But isn't the Mt. Baker district out of your way?"

"I do need to talk to your grandfather. There're some estimates I need to give him."

"But can't it wait until tomorrow? Honestly, Zach, you're exhausted. One day isn't going to make any difference. For that matter Gramps might not even be at the house."

Zach rubbed his eyes with the heels of his hands, then glanced irritably in her direction. "Honestly, Janine," he mocked, "you're beginning to sound like a wife already."

Biting her tongue to keep back her angry retort, Janine crossed her arms and glared out the side window. Indignation seeped through her with every breath she drew. Of its own accord, her foot started an impatient tapping. She could hardly wait to part company with this rude unreasonable man.

Apparently Zach didn't know when to quit, because he added, "Now you even look like one."

With a saccharine smile, she slowly turned to him and in an even more saccharine voice inquired, "And what's that supposed to mean?"

"Look at you, for heaven's sake. First you start nagging me and then—"

"Nagging you!" she exploded. "Let's get one thing straight, right now, Zachary Thomas. I do not nag."

Zach rolled his eyes, then turned his head to glare out the window on his side.

"Sir, sir," Janine said, sliding forward in the seat. She politely tapped the driver on the shoulder.

The middle-aged man with a deep receding hairline glanced at her. "What is it, lady?"

"Sir," she said, offering him her warmest, most sincere smile. "Tell me, do I look like the kind of woman who would nag?"

"Ah . . . Look, lady, all I do is drive a cab. You can ask me where a street is and I can tell you. If you want to go uptown, I can take you uptown. But when it comes to answering personal-type questions, I prefer to mind my own business."

"Are you satisfied?" Zach murmured.

"No, I'm not." She crossed her arms once more and stared straight ahead.

The cabdriver's eyes met hers in the rearview mirror, and Janine tried to smile, but when she caught a glimpse of herself, she realized her effort looked more like a grimace.

"Me and the Mrs. been married for near twenty years now," the driver said suddenly, stopping at a red light just off the James Street exit. "Me and the Mrs. managed to stay married through the good times and the bad. Can't say that about a lot of folks."

"I don't suppose your wife is the type who nags, though, is she?" Zach made the question sound more like a statement, sending Janine a look that rankled.

"Betsy does her fair share. If you ask me, nagging's just part of a woman's nature."

"That's ridiculous," Janine countered stiffly. She should have known better than to draw a complete stranger into the discussion, especially another male who was sure to take Zach's side.

"I'll tell you the real reason me and the missus managed to stay together all these years," the cabbie continued in a confiding tone. "We never go to bed angry at each other. I know I look like an easygoing kind of guy, but I've got a temper on me. Over the years, me and Betsy have had our share of fights, but we always kiss and make up."

Janine smiled and nodded, sorry she'd ever gotten involved in this conversation.

"Go on," the cabbie urged.

Janine's puzzled gaze briefly met Zach's.

"Go on and do what?" Zach wanted to know.

"Kiss and make up." The cabbie turned to smile at them and wink at Janine. "If my wife was as pretty as yours, mister, I wouldn't be hesitating."

He turned his attention back to his driving.

Janine nearly swallowed her tongue. "We are not married."

"And have no intention whatsoever of marrying," Zach added quickly.

The driver chuckled. "That's what they all say. The harder they deny it, the more in love they are."

He turned off Broadway and a few minutes later pulled into the circular driveway that led to Janine's house. As the talkative cabbie leapt out of the car and dashed for the trunk, Janine opened her door and climbed out.

Apparently, Zach had no intention of taking her advice, because he, too, got out of the cab. It was while they were tussling with the luggage that the front door opened and Mrs. McCormick hurried outside. Her white hair was tucked into a tight bun at the back of her head and she wore the ever present bib apron.

"Janine," she cried, her blue eyes lighting up with surprise. "What are you doing back so soon? We weren't expecting you for another two days."

"I missed your cooking so much, I couldn't bear to stay away any longer," Janine said, throwing her arms around the plump older woman in a warm hug. "Has Gramps been giving you any trouble?"

"Not a bit."

Zach paid the cabbie, who got back into the cab, but not before he'd winked at Janine again. "Remember what I told you," he yelled, backing out of the driveway and speeding off.

"How much was the fare?" Janine asked, automatically opening her purse.

"I took care of it," Zach said, reaching for his garment bag and the heavier of Janine's two suitcases. He said it as though he expected an argument from her, but if that was the case, Janine didn't plan to give him one.

"Is Gramps home?" Janine curved her arm affectionately around the housekeeper's thick waist as she spoke.

"He went out real early this morning, but I'm expecting him back soon."

"Good," Zach mumbled, following them into the house.

"I imagine you're both starved," Mrs. McCormick said, heading toward the kitchen. "Give me a few minutes and I'll whip you up something that'll make you both glad you're home.''

Left alone with Zach once more, Janine wasn't sure what to say to him. They'd spent almost twenty-four hours in each other's company. They'd argued. They'd talked. They'd laughed. They'd kissed.

"Janine—"

"Zach—"

They spoke simultaneously, then exchanged nervous smiles.

"You first," Zach said, gesturing toward her.

"I...I just wanted to say thanks for everything. I'll be in touch," she said. "By phone," she quickly assured him. "So you don't need to worry about me dropping into the office unannounced."

He grinned sheepishly. "Remember, communication is the key."

"I agree one hundred percent."

They stood facing each other in the foyer. "You wanted to say something?" she prompted after a moment.

"Yes." Zach exhaled sharply, then drew a hand along the side of his jaw. "What that cabbie said is true—even for us. I don't want us to part with any bad feelings. I shouldn't have said what I did back there—about nagging. You don't nag, and I had no right to say you did."

"I overreacted." The last thing she'd expected from Zach was an apology. His eyes, dark and tender, held hers, and without even realizing what she was doing, Janine took a step forward. Zach met her and she was about to slip into his arms when the sound of the front door opening drove them apart.

"Janine," Anton cried, delighted. "Zach. My, my, this is a pleasant surprise." He chuckled softly as he removed his coat. "Tell me, was your tryst on the moors as romantic as I hoped?"

CHAPTER SIX

"OUR BEST BET is to present a united front," Janine said to Zach four days later. They'd met at her house early in the afternoon to outline their strategy. Gramps was gone for the day, but by the time he returned, Zach and Janine planned to be ready to talk him out of this marriage idea. The sooner Anton realized his ploy wasn't working, the better. Then they could both get on with their lives and forget this unfortunate episode.

"It's important that we stand up to him together," Janine explained when Zach didn't comment. From the moment he'd arrived, he'd given her the impression that he'd rather not be doing this. Well, she wasn't overjoyed about plotting against her grandfather, either, but in this instance it was necessary. "If we don't, I'm afraid Gramps will continue to play us against each other."

"I'm here, aren't I?" Zach grumbled, looking none too pleased. He certainly wasn't in one of his better moods.

"Listen, if you're going to act like this—"

"Like what?" he demanded, standing up slowly. He walked over to the silver tea service and poured himself a cup of coffee. When he'd finished, he ambled to the fireplace and leaned against the mantel.

"Like you're doing me a big favor," Janine elaborated.

"You're the one who's left *me* dangling for three days. Do you realize what I've been forced to endure? Anton kept giving me these smug smiles, looking so pleased with himself and the way things had worked out in Scotland. Yesterday he went so far as to mention the name of a good jeweler."

Before Janine could stop herself, she was on her feet, arms akimbo, glaring at Zach. "I thought you were going to call me! Weren't you the one who claimed communication is the key? Then it's as if you'd dropped off the face of the earth! And for your information, it hasn't exactly been a Sunday school picnic around here, either."

"It may surprise you to learn that I have other things on my mind besides dealing with you and your grandfather."

"Implying I don't have anything to do with *my* time?" she snapped.

"No," he said slowly, after a moment. "Damn it, Janine, we're arguing again."

She sighed regretfully. "I know. We've got to stop this infernal squabbling. It's counterproductive."

Zach's nod was curt and she saw that he was frowning. "What troubles me most is the way your grandfather found us the other day. We were standing so close and you were staring up at me with those baby blues of yours, silently begging me to kiss you."

"I most certainly was not," she denied, knowing Zach was right. Her cheeks grew pink. She *had* wanted him to kiss her, but she hated having to admit that she would have walked into his arms without a second's hesitation. It was best, she decided, to blame that un-expected longing on the exhausting flight home.

Zach shook his head and set his coffee cup carefully on the mantel. He thrust both hands into his pockets, still slouching against the fireplace wall. "The problem is, I was ready to do it. If your grandfather hadn't walked in when he did, I would have kissed you."

"You would?" she asked softly, feeling almost light-headed at his words.

Zach straightened, and a nerve in his jaw jerked, calling her attention to the strong chiseled lines of his face. "I'm only human," he said dryly. "I'll admit I'm as susceptible to a beautiful woman as the next man, especially when she all but asks me to take her in my arms."

That was too much. Janine pinched her lips together to keep from crying out in anger. Taking a moment to compose herself, she closed her eyes and drew in a deep calming breath. "Instead of blaming each other for something that *didn't happen*, could we please return to the subject at hand, which happens to be my grandfather?"

"All right," Zach agreed readily. "I apologize. I shouldn't have said anything." He walked to the wing-back leather chair and sat down. Leaning forward, he rested his elbows on his knees. "What do you think you should say to him?"

"Me? I thought . . . I'd hoped . . . you'd want to do the talking."

Zach shook his head. "Tact doesn't seem to be my strong point lately."

"Okay, okay, I'll do the talking, if that's what you really want." She gazed silently down at the richly patterned carpet, collecting her thoughts. "I think we should say something about how much we both love and respect him and that we realize his actions have been motivated by his concern for us both and his desire for our happiness. We might even go so far as to thank him—" She stopped abruptly when Zach gave a snort of laughter. "All right, if you think you could do any better, you do the talking."

"If it was up to me I'd just tell that meddling old fool to stay out of our lives."

"Your sensitivity is really heartwarming," she muttered. "First this whole thing was one big joke to you, and you really enjoyed tormenting me."

"You're exaggerating."

"As I recall you played that cow-and-ten-chickens business for all it was worth, but I notice you're singing a different tune now and frankly—"

The library door opened, interrupting her tirade. Her grandfather and his longtime friend, veterinarian Dr. Burt Coleman, walked into the room, unaware that Janine and Zach were inside.

"Zach. Janine," Gramps said, grinning broadly.

"Gramps," Janine burst out, rushing to her feet. They weren't prepared for this, and Zach was being impossible, so she said the first thing that came to mind. Pointing at Zach, she cried, "I don't know how you could possibly expect me to marry that man. He's stubborn and rude and we're completely wrong for each other." She was trembling by the time she finished, and collapsed gracelessly into the nearest chair.

"In case you haven't figured it out yet, you're no angel yourself," Zach growled, glaring at Janine.

"Children, please," Gramps implored, advancing into the library, hands held out in supplication. "What seems to be the problem?"

"I want the subject settled once and for all," Zach said forcefully. "I'm not about to be saddled with Janine for a wife."

"And I want to be *your* wife? In your dreams, Zachary Thomas!"

"We realize you mean well," Zach added, his face looking pinched. He completely ignored Janine. "But neither of us appreciates your matchmaking efforts."

Gramps walked over to the leather chair recently occupied by Zach and sat down. He smiled weakly at each of them, his shoulders sagging. "I thought...I'd hoped you two would grow fond of each other."

"You mean if we don't murder each other first," Zach grumbled.

"I'm sorry to disappoint you, Gramps, I really am," Janine said, feeling wretched. "But Zach and I don't even like each other. We can barely carry on a civil conversation. He's argumentative and unreasonable—"

"And she's illogical and stubborn."

"I don't think we need to trade insults to get our message across," Janine said stiffly. Her face was so hot, she felt as if her cheeks were on fire.

"There's no hope?" Anton's expression altered, as if he were in pain.

"None whatsoever," Zach said, his voice surprisingly even. "I'm sure Janine will make some man a wonderful wife one day, but unfortunately, he won't be me."

Her grandfather slumped against the back of his chair. "You're sure?"

"Positive," Zach said, loud enough to convince Mrs. McCormick who was working in the kitchen.

"I love you, Gramps," said Janine, "and I'd do most anything you wanted, but I can't and won't marry Zach. We realize you have our best interests at heart, but neither of us is romantically interested in the other."

Burt Coleman remained just inside the library, looking as if he'd rather be anyplace else. His discomfort at witnessing this family scene was obvious. "I think it'd be best if I came back another time," he murmured as he turned to leave.

"No," Anton argued, gesturing his friend back. "Come in. You know Zachary Thomas, don't you?"

The two men nodded toward each other, but Janine noticed how rigidly Zach held himself. This meeting with Gramps hadn't gone the way she'd hoped or planned. She'd wanted everything to be calm and rational, a discussion uncluttered by messy emotions. Instead they'd ended up practically attacking each other, and worse, Janine had been the one to throw the first punch.

Without asking, she walked over to the tea service and poured Gramps and his friend a cup of hot coffee. Burt sat across from her grandfather, clearly ill at ease at being thrust into this awkward situation.

"I should be going," Zach announced starkly. "Good to see you again, Dr. Coleman."

"You, too," Gramps's friend said, glancing briefly toward Zach. His puzzled gaze quickly returned to Anton.

"I'll walk you to the front door," Janine said, eager to make her own escape. She closed the library door behind her.

Both she and Zach paused in the entryway. Janine tried to smile, but Zach was staring at her steadily, and her heart clenched like a fist inside her chest. They'd done what they had to do; she should be experiencing relief that the confrontation she'd dreaded for days was finally over. Instead she felt a strange sadness, one she couldn't fully understand or explain.

"Do you think we convinced him?"

"I don't know," Zach answered, keeping his tone low. "Your grandfather's a difficult man to read. It could be he'll never bring up the subject of our marrying again and we're home free. I'd like to think that's the case. Just as likely, though, he'll give us a few days' peace while he regroups. I don't expect him to give up quite so easily."

"No, I don't suppose he will."

Zach looked at his watch. "I should be going," he said again.

Janine was reluctant to see him leave, but there wasn't any reason to detain him. Her hand was on the doorknob when she suddenly hesitated and turned around. "I didn't mean what I said in there," she blurted in a frenzy of regret.

"You mean you do want us to marry?"

"No," she cried, aghast. "I'm talking about when I said you were stubborn and rude. That isn't entirely true, but I had to come up with some reason for finding you so objectionable. But I don't really believe it."

"It was the same with me. I don't find you so intolerable, either. I was trusting that you knew it was all an act for your grandfather's sake."

"I did," she assured him, but her pride *had* been dented, though that wasn't anything new.

"The last four days have been difficult at best," Zach went on. "Not only was Anton gloating about Scotland, but like I told you, he's been giving me these amused looks and odd little smiles. A couple of times I heard him murmuring something in his native tongue—I'm afraid to guess what."

"Well, I know what he was saying, because he's been doing the same thing to me. He's talking about babies."

"Babies?" Zach echoed, his eyes round and startled.

"Ours in particular."

"Good Lord." One corner of Zach's mouth lifted, as if he found the thought of them as parents amusing. Or unlikely.

"That was my reaction, too. Every time I've seen Gramps in the last few days, he's started talking about . . . well, you know."

Zach nodded. "I do know. Things haven't been pleasant for either of us."

"Our setting Gramps straight was for the best." But if that was the case, why did she feel this terrible letdown? "If he accepts us at our word, and he just might, then I guess this is goodbye."

"Yes, I suppose it is," Zach responded, but he made no effort to leave.

Janine was glad, because these few moments gave her the opportunity to memorize his proud sharp features. She stored them for the future, when there would be no reason for her to have anything but the most infrequent contact with Zach.

"Unless, of course, your grandfather continues to find ways to throw us together."

"Of course," Janine added quickly, hating the way her heart soared at the prospect. "Naturally, we'd be forced to confront him again. We can't allow ourselves to be his pawns."

Zach was about to say something more, when the library door flew open and Burt Coleman hurried out, the urgency on his face unmistakable. "Janine, I think we should call a doctor for your grandfather."

"What's wrong?"

"I'm not sure. He's gone terribly pale and he seems to be having trouble breathing. I think it might be his heart."

With Zach following, Janine ran into the library, her own heart in jeopardy. Dr. Coleman was right— she'd never seen her grandfather look worse. His breath came noisily and his eyes were closed as he rested his head against the back of the chair. He looked old, far older than she could ever remember seeing him. A sense of panic filled her as she raced across the room to the desk where there was a phone.

"I'm fine," Gramps said hoarsely, opening his eyes and slowly straightening. He raised his hand in an effort to stop Janine. "There's no need for everyone to go into a tizzy just because an old man wants to rest his eyes for a few minutes." His smile was weak, his complexion still pale. "Now don't go calling any doctor. I was in last week for a checkup and I'm fit as a fiddle."

"You don't look so fit," Zach countered and Janine noted that his face seemed almost as ashen as her grandfather's. Kneeling beside the older man, Zach grasped his wrist and began to check his pulse.

"I'm fine," Gramps insisted.

"Are you in any pain?"

Gramps's gaze moved from his partner to Janine. "None," he answered, dismissing their concern with a short hard shake of his head.

"Dr. Coleman?" Janine looked to her grandfather's longtime friend. "Should I phone his doctor?"

"What does Burt know about an old man and his heart?" Gramps objected. "Burt's expertise is with horses."

"Call the doctor. Having him checked over isn't going to hurt," Burt said after a moment.

"Fiddlesticks," Gramps roared. "I'm in perfect health."

"Good," Janine said brightly. "But I'll just let Dr. Madison reassure me." She punched out the phone number and had to speak loudly in order to be heard over her grandfather's protests. A couple of minutes later, she replaced the receiver and told Zach, "Dr. Madison says we can bring him in now."

"I'm not going to waste valuable time traipsing downtown. Burt and I were going to play a few hands of cribbage."

"We can play tomorrow," Dr. Coleman said gruffly. "You keep forgetting, Anton, we're retiring."

"I've got things to do at the office."

"No, you don't," Zach said firmly. "You've got a doctor's appointment. Janine and I are going to escort you there and we aren't going to listen to a single argument. Do you understand?"

Gramps's gaze narrowed as if he were preparing a loud rebuttal. But he apparently changed his mind, because he relaxed and nodded sluggishly, reluctantly. "All right, if it'll make you feel better. But I'm telling you right now, you're going to look like a fine pair of fools."

The next two hours felt like two years to Janine. While Dr. Madison examined Gramps, she and Zach paced the waiting room. Several patients came and went.

"What could be taking so long?" Janine asked, wringing her hands nervously. "Do you think we did the right thing bringing him here? I mean, should we have gone directly to the hospital emergency room instead?"

"I doubt he would have agreed to that," Zach said.

"Do you honestly believe I would have listened to him?" She sat on the edge of a chair and gripped her hands together so tightly her knuckles whitened. "It's ridiculous, but I've never thought of Gramps as old. He's always been so healthy, so alive. I've never once considered what would happen if he were to become ill."

"He's going to be fine, Janine."

"You saw him," she cried, struggling against the dread and horror that churned inside her.

Zach's hand clasped hers and the fears that had torn at her composure only seconds earlier seemed to abate with his touch. He lent her confidence and strength, and she was badly in need of both.

When the door leading to the doctor's office opened, they both leapt to their feet. Zach's hand tightened around hers before he released it.

"Dr. Madison can talk to you now," the nurse told them briskly. She led the way to a compact office and explained that the doctor would be with them in a few minutes. Janine sat in one of the thickly cushioned chairs and ran her gaze over the framed degrees on the walls.

Dr. Madison came into the room moments later. He paused to shake hands with Zach and nod politely toward Janine. "My tests don't show anything we need to be too concerned about," he said, shuffling through the papers on his desk.

"What happened? Why was he so pale? Why was he gasping like that?" Janine demanded.

Dr. Madison frowned and folded his hands. "I really couldn't say. He claims he hadn't been doing any strenuous exercise."

"No, he was drinking coffee and talking to a friend when it happened."

Dr. Madison nodded. "Did he recently receive any negative news regarding his business?"

"No," Janine replied, glancing at Zach. "If anything, the business is doing better than ever. Gramps is getting ready to retire. I hate the thought of anything happening to him now."

"I don't know what to tell you," Dr. Madison said with a thoughtful frown. "He should take it easy for the next couple of days, but there's nothing to worry about that I can find."

Janine sighed and closed her eyes. "Thank God."

"Your grandfather's getting dressed now," Dr. Madison said. He stood, signaling the end of their interview. "He'll join you in a few minutes."

"Thank you, Doctor," Zach said fervently.

Relief washed through Janine like a tidal wave. She got up and smiled at Zach. It was a smile full of gratitude. A smile one might share with a good friend when something has gone unexpectedly right. The kind of smile a woman would share with her husband. The thought hit her full force and she quickly lowered her gaze to cover her reaction.

When Gramps joined them in the waiting room, he looked immeasurably better. His blue eyes were filled with indignation and his skin tone was a healthy pink. "I hope the pair of you are satisfied," he said huskily, buttoning his coat. "The better part of the afternoon was wasted with this nonsense."

"You were a hundred percent right, Gramps," Janine said brightly. "You're as fit as a fiddle and we wasted valuable cribbage time dragging you down here."

"I should have been back at the office hours ago," Zach put in, sharing a smile with Janine.

"And whose fault is that?" Anton demanded. He brushed off his sleeves as though he'd been forced to pick himself up off the floor, no thanks to them.

Once more Janine and Zach shared an intimate look. They both seemed to realize at the same moment what they were doing and abruptly glanced away.

Zach drove Gramps and Janine back to the house, Gramps protesting loudly all the while that they'd overreacted and ruined his afternoon. His first concern seemed to be rescheduling his cribbage game.

Janine walked Zach back to his car. "Thanks for everything," she said, folding her arms around her middle to repress the sudden urge to hug him.

"If you're worried about anything, give me a call," Zach said as he opened the car door. He hesitated fractionally, then lifted his head and gazed directly into her eyes. "Goodbye, Janine."

She raised her hand in farewell and a sadness settled over her. "Goodbye, Zach," she said forcing a lightness into her voice. "Thanks again."

For the longest moment, he said nothing, although his eyes still held hers. Finally he repeated, "Call me if you need anything, all right?"

"I will."

But they both knew she wouldn't. It was best to end this now. Make a clean cut.

Janine stood in the driveway until Zach's car was well out of sight. Only then did she return to the house.

"THIS IS REALLY GOOD of you," Patty St. John whispered, handing the sleeping infant to Janine. "I don't know what I would've done if I'd had to drag Michael to the interview. I need this job so badly."

"I'm happy to help." Janine peered down at the sweet face of the sleeping six-month-old baby. "I apologize if it was inconvenient for you to bring Michael here, but I've been sticking close to the house for the past few days. My grandfather hasn't been feeling well."

"It isn't any problem," Patty whispered, setting the diaper bag on the floor. She glanced around the house. "This place is really something. I didn't have any idea that you...well, you know, that you were so well off."

"This house belongs to my grandfather," Janine explained, gently rocking Michael in her arms. The warmth and tenderness she felt toward the baby was a revelation. It was understandable, though, when she thought about it. Gramps had spent last week constantly telling her what remarkable babies she and Zach would have, and here she was with one in her arms. All the maternal instincts she didn't know she had came bubbling to the surface.

"I'll be back in about an hour," Patty said. She leaned over and kissed Michael's soft forehead. He didn't so much as stir.

Still carrying the baby, Janine walked to the door with her friend. "Good luck."

Patty gave a strained smile and crossed her fingers. "Thanks. I'm going to need it."

No sooner had the door closed when Anton walked into the living room. He paused when he saw Janine gently rocking in the old chair that had once belonged to his wife. His face relaxed into a broad grin.

"Is that a baby you've got there?"

Janine smiled. "Nothing gets past you, does it, Gramps?"

He chuckled. "Who's he belong to?"

"Patty St. John. You might remember my mentioning her. She's another volunteer at the Friendship Club. She quit her job when Michael was born, but now she'd like to find some part-time work."

"Are you volunteering to baby-sit for her?"

"Just for today," Janine explained. "Her regular sitter has the flu."

"I thought you were going out?" Gramps muttered, with a slight frown. "You haven't left the house all week. Fact is, you're becoming a recluse."

"I've had other things to do," she returned, not raising her voice for fear of disturbing the baby.

"Right. The other things you had to do were keep an eye on your grandfather," he protested. "You think I didn't notice? How long do you plan on being my shadow? You should be gadding about, doing the things you normally do, instead of worrying yourself sick over me. I'm fine, I tell you. When are you going to listen to me?''

"Dr. Madison said to keep an eye on you for a few days."

"It's been a week."

Janine didn't need her grandfather to tell her that. She was beginning to suffer from cabin fever. She'd spoken to hardly anyone all week. She hadn't heard from Zach, either. Not that she'd expected to. Perhaps Gramps had taken them at their word. Or else he was doing what Zach had suspected and simply regrouping for the next skirmish.

Michael stirred in her arms and she gently placed him against her shoulder, rocking him back to sleep.

"I'm going to the office tomorrow," Gramps announced, eyeing her defiantly as though he anticipated a challenge.

"We'll see," she said, delaying the showdown.

Yawning, baby Michael raised his head and looked around. Gramps's weathered face broke into a tender smile. "All right," he agreed easily. "We'll see." He offered the little boy his finger and Michael gripped it firmly in his hand, then started to chew on it.

Janine laughed, watching her grandfather react to the baby. After a couple of minutes, Michael grew tired of the game with Anton's finger and yawned again, arching his back. Janine decided it was time to check his diaper. She got up, reaching for the bag Patty had left.

"I'll be back in a minute," she told her grandfather.

She was halfway across the living room when Anton stopped her. "You look real good with a baby in your arms. Natural."

Janine smiled. She didn't dare let him know how right it felt to hold one.

While she was changing the baby, she heard the doorbell ring. Normally she would have answered it herself, but since she was busy, either Gramps or Mrs. McCormick would see to it.

Michael was happily investigating his toes and making cooing sounds as Janine pulled up his rubber pants. "You're going to have to be patient with me, kiddo," she told him, carefully untwisting the legs of his corduroy overalls and snapping them back in place. When she'd finished, she lifted him high above her head and laughed when Michael squealed delightedly. They were both smiling when she returned to the living room.

Gramps was sitting in the chair closest to the grand piano, and across from him sat Zach.

Janine's heart lurched as her eyes instantly flew to Zach's. The laughter drained out of her. "Hello, Zach," she said, striving to sound as nonchalant as possible, tucking Michael against her hip. She cast a suspicious glare at her grandfather, who smiled back, the picture of innocence.

"Zach brought some papers for me to sign," Gramps explained.

"I didn't mean to interrupt you," she apologized. Her gaze refused to leave Zach's. He smiled that slanted half-smile of his that wasn't really a smile at all. The one she'd always found so appealing. Something seemed to pass between them—a tenderness, a hunger.

"Janine's not interrupting anything, is she?" Gramps asked.

"No," Zach responded gruffly. He seemed to be taking in everything about her, from the acid-washed jeans and oversize pink shirt to the gurgling baby riding so casually on her hip.

Gramps cleared his throat. "If you'll excuse me a moment, I'll go get a pen," he said, leaving them alone together.

"How have you been?" Zach asked, his eyes riveted to her.

"Fine. Just fine."

"I see you haven't had any problems finding another admirer," he murmured, nodding at Michael.

Zach kept his tone light and teasing, and Janine followed his lead. "Michael St. John," she said, turning slightly to give Zach a better view of the baby, "meet Mr. Thomas."

"Hello," Zach said, holding up his palm. He looked questionably awkward around children. "I take it you're watching him for a friend."

"Yes, another volunteer. She's looking for a part-time job, but there's a problem finding one with the right hours. She's at an interview."

"I see."

Janine sank down on the ottoman in front of Zach's chair and set Michael on her knee. She focused her attention on gently bouncing the baby. "Now that your life is back in order," she said playfully, glancing up at Zach, "have you discovered how much you miss me?"

He chuckled softly. "It's been how long since we last talked? Seven days? I'm telling you, Janine, I haven't had a single disagreement with anyone in all that time."

"That should make you happy."

"You're right. It should." He shook his head. "Unfortunately it doesn't. Damn it all, Janine, I was bored to death. So the answer is yes, I missed you."

CHAPTER SEVEN

BEFORE JANINE HAD A CHANCE to respond, Gramps wandered back into the living room, pen in hand.

"You said you had some papers you wanted me to sign," Anton reminded Zach.

With obvious reluctance, Zach tore his gaze from Janine's. He opened his briefcase and brought out several papers. "Go ahead and read these over."

"Do you need me to sign them or not?" her grandfather grumbled.

Once more Zach dragged his gaze away from Janine. "Sure, go ahead."

Muttering under his breath, Gramps took the documents to the small table, scanned them and quickly scrawled his name.

Janine knew she should leave; the two men probably wanted to discuss business. But she couldn't make herself stand up and walk away. Not when Zach had actually admitted that he'd missed her.

Gramps broke into her thoughts. "Janine, I—"

"I was just going," she said quickly. She clambered to her feet, securing her hold on Michael.

But Gramps surprised her.

"I want you to stay," he declared. "I wanted to talk to you and Zach. Fact is, I owe you both an apology. Burt and I had a good long talk the other day and I told him how I'd tried to arrange a marriage between the two of you. He laughed and called me an old fool, claimed it was time I stepped out of the Dark Ages."

"Gramps," Janine said anxiously, unwilling to discuss the subject that had brought such contention, "Zach and I have already settled that issue. We realize why you did it and . . . and we've laid it to rest, so there's no need to apologize."

"I'm afraid there is," Gramps insisted. "Don't worry, Burt pointed out the error of my ways. Haven't got any new tricks up my sleeve." He rose to bring Zach the signed papers, then sat wearily in the chair across from them. He'd never looked so fragile, so old and beaten.

"Janine's a wonderful woman," Zach said unexpectedly. "I want you to know I realize that."

"She's got her faults," Gramps responded, reaching for a cigar, "but she's pretty enough to compensate."

"Thank you very much," Janine whispered sarcastically and was rewarded with an off-center grin from Zach. Gramps didn't seem to hear her; if he had, he was ignoring her comment.

"I only want the best for her, but when I approached her about marrying you, she put up a big fuss. Fact is, it would have been easier to pluck a live chicken. When it came right down to it, she said she needed *romance*." Gramps pronounced the word as if it were one that evoked instant amusement.

"There isn't a woman alive who doesn't need romance," she wailed, defending herself.

"I'm from the old country," Gramps continued. "Romance wasn't something I knew about from personal experience, and when I asked Janine to explain, she had some trouble defining it herself. Said it was a tryst on the moors and a bunch of other hogwash. That's the reason I sent you both to Scotland.''

"We figured that out soon enough," Zach said dryly.

"As you'll recall," Janine found herself rejoining, "that definition was off the top of my head. I'll have you know romance isn't easy to explain, especially to a man who scoffs at the entire idea."

Anton chuckled, moving the cigar to the side of his mouth. "It's unfortunate the two of you caught on to me so soon. I was looking forward to arranging the desperate passion part."

"Desperate passion?" Zach echoed.

"Yes. Janine said that was all part of romance, too. I may be over seventy, but I know about passion. Oh, yes, Anna and I learned about that together." His blue eyes took on a faraway look and his lips curved in the gentlest of smiles. He glanced at Janine and his smile widened.

"I'm pleased you find this so amusing," Janine snapped.

Gramps dismissed her anger with a flick of his hand and looked at Zach. "I suppose you've discovered she's got something of a temper?"

"From the start!" Zach declared.

"It may come as a surprise to you, Zachary Thomas," said Janine, "but you're not exactly Mr. Perfect."

"No," Zach countered smoothly. "I think your grandfather was thinking more along the lines of Mr. Right."

"Oh, brother!"

"Now, children, I don't see that arguing will do any good. I've willingly accepted defeat. Trying to interest you in each other was an old man's way of setting his world right before he passes on.''

The doorbell chimed and, grateful for an excuse to leave the room, Janine hurried to answer it. Patty St. John stood there, her face cheerless, her posture forlorn.

"I wasn't expecting you back nearly so soon."

"They'd already hired someone," Patty explained, walking into the foyer and automatically taking her son from Janine. She held the infant close, as if his small warm body might absorb her disappointment. "I spent the entire day psyching myself up for this interview and it was all for nothing. Ah, well, who wants to be a receptionist at a dental clinic, anyway?"

"I'm so sorry," Janine murmured.

"Was Michael any problem?"

"None at all," Janine assured her, wishing she could think of something encouraging to say. "I'll get his things for you."

It took Janine only a minute to collect Michael's diaper bag, but when she returned to the entryway, she discovered Zach talking to Patty. Janine saw him hand her friend his business card and overheard him suggesting she report to the personnel office early the following week.

"Thanks again," Patty said enthusiastically to both of them. She lifted Michael's hand. "Say bye-bye," she coaxed the baby, then raised his arm and moved it for him.

Janine let her out, with Zach standing next to her. Gramps had gone into the library, and Zach glanced anxiously in that direction before lowering his voice to a whisper. "Can you meet me later?"

"When?"

"In an hour." He checked his watch, then mentioned the number of a pier along the waterfront. Janine had just managed to clarify the location when Gramps returned.

Zach left the house soon afterward and Janine was able to come up with an excuse half an hour later. Gramps was reading and didn't bother to look up from his mystery novel, although Janine suspected she saw the hint of a smile, as if he knew full well what she was up to. She didn't linger to investigate. The last time she'd agreed to a clandestine meeting with Zach had been the night they'd met at the Italian restaurant, when she'd all but blurted out the arrangements to her grandfather.

Zach was waiting for her, grim-faced. He stood against the pier railing, the wind whipping his raincoat against his legs.

"I hope there's a good reason for this, because I don't think Gramps is a fool," Janine announced when she joined him. "He'll more than likely figure out that I'm meeting you if I'm not back soon." She buried her hands in her jacket pockets, turning away from the wind. The afternoon sky was gray, threatening rain.

"Am I interrupting something important?"

"Not really." Janine wouldn't have minded listing several pressing engagements, but she'd canceled everything for the next two weeks, wanting to stay close to home in case her grandfather needed her.

Zach clasped his hands behind his back and started strolling down the pier the wind ruffling his neatly trimmed hair. Janine followed. "I'm worried about Anton," he said suddenly, stopping and facing Janine.

"Why?" Perhaps there was something she didn't know about his health, something Dr. Madison hadn't told her.

"He doesn't look good."

"How do you mean?" Although she asked, she already knew the answer. She'd felt the same thing the past few days. Gramps was aging right before her eyes.

"I think you know."

"I do," she admitted reluctantly.

"Furthermore I'm worried about you."

"Me?" she asked, her voice rising. "Whatever for?"

"If, God forbid, anything should happen to Anton," Zach said, drawing in a ragged breath, "what will happen to you? You don't have any other family, do you?"

"No," she told him, her chest tightening at the thought. "But I'm not worried about it. There are several friends who are very close to the family, Burt Coleman for one, so I wouldn't be cast into the streets like an orphan. There's no need for you to be concerned. I'm not."

"I see." Zach frowned as he walked to the farthest end of the pier, seeming to fix his gaze on the snow-capped peaks of the Olympic mountains far in the distance.

Janine hurried to catch up with him. "Why do you ask?" she demanded.

"He's always said he was concerned about your not having any other family. But it wasn't until recently that I really understood some of his motivations in trying to arrange a marriage between us."

"Good, then you can explain it to me, because frankly, I'm at a loss. He admitted he was wrong, but

I don't think he's given up on the idea. He'd do just about anything to see the two of us together.''

"I *know* he hasn't given up on us."

"What did he do? Up the ante?"

Zach chuckled and his features relaxed into a smile as he met her eyes. "Nothing so explicit. He simply told me that he's getting on in years and hates the thought of you being left so alone when he dies."

"I'll adjust. I'm not a child," she insisted, although her heart filled with dread at the thought of life without her cantankerous, generous-hearted grandfather.

"I don't doubt you would." Zach hesitated, then resumed strolling, apparently taking it for granted that she'd continue to follow him.

"I have plenty of friends."

Zach nodded, although Janine was certain he hadn't heard her. He stopped abruptly and turned to look at her. "What I'm about to say is going to shock you."

Janine stared up at him, not knowing what to expect.

"When you think about it, our getting married makes an odd kind of sense."

"What?" Janine couldn't believe what she was hearing.

"From a practical point of view," he rushed to explain. "With the business in both our names, plus the fact that we're both alone. I realize I'm not exactly Prince Charming..." Zach paused as if he expected her to contradict him. When she didn't, he frowned but eventually continued, "The problem has more to do with whether we can get along. I don't even know if we're capable of going an entire day without arguing."

"What are you suggesting?" Janine asked, wondering if she was reading more into this conversation than he intended.

"Nothing yet. Frankly, I'm trying to be as open and as honest as I can and it's damn difficult." He gripped the railing with both hands and braced himself, as though expecting a fierce wind to uproot him.

"Are you thinking that our getting married wouldn't be such a bad idea after all?" Janine ventured. Initially he'd made a joke of the whole thing, infuriating her. Then he'd seen it as an annoyance. Now he seemed to have changed his mind again.

"I...don't know yet. I'm mulling over my thoughts, which I'm willing to confess are hopelessly tangled at the moment."

"Mine aren't much better."

"Does this mean you'd consider the possibility?"

"I don't know." Janine had thought she was in love once. She remembered how Brian had gently wooed her, how he'd done everything a romantic hero should do. He'd sent her flowers, said all the things a woman longs to hear and then, without a pause, he'd casually broken her heart. When she thought about it now, she couldn't really imagine herself married to Brian. But Zach, who'd never made any romantic gestures, seemed somehow to fit into her life almost naturally. And yet...

As she pondered these contradictions, Zach started walking again. "I realize I'm not the kind of husband you want," he was saying, "and not near as good as you deserve. I'd like to be the man of your dreams, but I'm not. Nor am I likely to change at this stage of my life." He paused, chancing a look in her direction. "What are you thinking?"

Janine sighed and concentrated as hard as she could, but her mind was filled with so many questions, so many doubts. "Would you mind very much kissing me?"

Shock widened his dark eyes. He glanced around, then scowled. "Now? Right here?"

"Yes."

"There are people everywhere. Is this really necessary?"

"Would I ask you to do it if it weren't?"

As he searched her face, she moistened her lips and looked up at him, tilting her head slightly. Slowly, reluctantly, Zach slipped one arm around her waist and drew her close. Her heart reacted immediately, leaping into a hard fast rhythm that made her feel slightly breathless. He lifted her chin with his free hand and slowly lowered his mouth to hers.

The instant his lips grazed hers, Janine was flooded with a sensual languor. It was as if they'd returned to the moors of Scotland with the full moon overhead pouring magic onto their small corner of the earth. Everything around them faded. No longer did Janine hear the sound of water slapping against the wooden columns of the pier. The blustery day went calm.

She supported her hands on his chest, breathing erratically, when he stopped kissing her. Neither spoke. Janine wanted to, but none of her faculties seemed to be working at the moment. She parted her lips and Zach lowered his mouth to hers once more. Only this time it was a full-fledged kiss, deep and probing. His hands slid up her back as his mouth abandoned hers to explore the sweep of her neck.

Several glorious moments passed before he shuddered, raised his head and drew back slightly, although he continued to hold her. "Does that answer your question?"

"No," she answered, hating the way her voice trembled. "I'm afraid it only raised more."

"I know what you mean," Zach admitted, briefly closing his eyes. "This last week apart was something of an eye-opener for me. I thought I'd be glad to put this matter between your grandfather and us to rest. If you want the truth, I thought I'd be glad to be rid of you. I was convinced you felt the same way." He paused, waiting for some kind of response from her.

"The days seemed so empty," she whispered.

His eyes burned into hers, and he nodded his head. "You were constantly on my mind, and I found myself wishing you were there to talk to." He groaned. "Heaven knows you deserve a different kind of husband than I could possibly be."

"What about you? I've heard you say a hundred times that when it comes to finding a wife, you'll choose your own."

He blinked, as though he didn't recognize his own words for a moment. Then he shrugged. "Once I got to know you, I realized you're not so bad."

"Thanks." So much for wine and roses and sweet nothings whispered in her ear. But then again, she'd had those things and they hadn't brought her happiness.

"I hate to admit it, but our getting married makes sense. We seem to like each other well enough, and there's a certain...attraction." Zach was frowning a little as he spoke. "It would be a good move for both of us from a financial viewpoint, as well." He gripped her by the shoulders and gazed into her eyes. "The question is, Janine, can I make you happy?"

Her heart melted at the way he said it, at the simplicity, the sincerity of his words. "What about you? Will you be content being married to me?"

The apprehension in his face eased. "I think so. We'll be good for each other. This isn't any grand passion. But I'm fond of you and you're fond of me."

"Fond?" Janine repeated, breaking away.

"What's wrong with that?"

"I hate that word," Janine said through gritted teeth. "Fond sounds so watered down...so weak. I'm not looking for a grand passion, as you put it, but I want a whole lot more than *fond*." She gestured dramatically with her hands. "A man is fond of his dog or a favorite place to eat, not his wife." She spoke so vehemently that she was starting to attract attention from other strollers. "Would it be too much for you to come up with another word?"

"Stop looking at me as if it were a matter of life and death," he said.

"It's important," she insisted.

Zach looked distinctly uncomfortable. "I run a business. There are more than a hundred outlets in fifty states. I know the office-supply business inside out, but I'm not good with words. If you don't like the word *fond*, you choose another one."

"All right," she said thoughtfully, biting the corner of one lip. Her eyes brightened. "How about cherish?"

"Cherish." Zach repeated it as if he'd never heard the word before. "Okay, it's a deal. I'll cherish you."

"And I'll cherish you," she said emphatically, nodding with satisfaction.

They walked along the pier until they came to a seafood stand, where Zach bought them each a cup of steaming clam chowder. They found an unoccupied picnic table and sat down, side by side.

Occasionally they stopped eating to smile at each other. An oddly exciting sensation attacked Janine's stomach every time that happened. Finally, finishing her soup, she licked the back of the white plastic spoon. She kept her eyes carefully lowered as she said, "I want to make sure I understand. Did we or did we not just agree to get married?"

Zach hesitated, his spoon halfway between his cup and his mouth as an odd, still look crossed his face. He swallowed once. "We decided to go through with it, both realizing this isn't the traditional love match, but one based on practical and financial advantages."

Janine dropped her spoon into the plastic cup. "If that's the case, the wedding's off."

Zach threw back his head and stared into the sky. "Now, what did I say that was so terrible?"

"Financial and practical advantages! You make the whole thing sound as appealing as a dentist appointment. There's got to be more reason than that for us to marry."

Shrugging, Zach gestured helplessly with his hands. "I already told you I wasn't any good at this. Perhaps we'd do better if you explained why you're willing to marry me."

She hesitated and before she could prevent it, a smile tugged at the corners of her mouth. "You won't like my reason any better than I like yours." She looked all around to be sure no one could overhear, then leaned toward him. "When we kissed a few minutes ago, the earth moved. I know it's a dreadful cliché, but that's exactly what I felt."

"The earth moved," Zach repeated deadpan.

"It happened when we were in Scotland, too. I don't know what's going on between us or even if we're doing the right thing, but there's definitely... something, something special."

She wasn't surprised when Zach scowled. "You mean to say you're willing to marry me because I'm a good kisser?"

"It makes a whole lot more sense to me than that stuff about financial advantages."

"You were absolutely correct," he said evenly. "I don't like your reason. Is there anything else that makes the prospect appealing?"

Janine giggled. "You know," she reflected, "Gramps was right. We're going to be very good for each other."

A flash of light warmed his eyes and his hand reached for hers. He entwined their fingers as their eyes met. "Yes, we are."

THE WEDDING WAS ARRANGED so fast that Janine barely had time to reconsider their decision. They applied for a license that same afternoon. When they returned to the house, Gramps shouted for joy, slapped Zach across the back several times and repeatedly hugged Janine, claiming she'd made an old man happy.

Janine was so busy, the days and nights soon mingled together and she lost all track of time. There were so many things to do—fittings and organizing caterers and inviting guests—that for the following five days she didn't so much as talk to Zach even once.

The day before the ceremony, the garden was buzzing with activity. Mrs. McCormick was busy supervising the men who were assembling the wedding canopy and setting up the tables and chairs.

Exhausted, Janine wandered outside and glanced toward the bold blue sky, praying the sunshine would hold for at least another day. The lawn was lush and green, and freshly mowed. The roses were in bloom, perfuming the air with their rich fragrance.

"Janine."

She recognized his voice immediately. She turned around to discover Zach striding purposely toward her, and her heart reacted of its own accord. She felt as though they'd been apart for a year instead of just a few days. She wore jeans and a sweatshirt and wished now that she'd chosen something less casual. In contrast, Zach was strikingly formal, dressed in a handsome pin-striped suit and dark tie. She was willing to admit she didn't know him as well as she should—as well as a woman who was about to become his wife. His habits, his likes and dislikes, were a mystery to her, yet those details seemed minor. It was the inner Zach she was coming to understand. The little she'd learned was enough to assure her that she'd made the right decision.

"Hello," she called, walking toward him. She noted that he looked as tired as she felt. Apparently he'd been just as busy, though the wedding preparations had been left to her.

They met halfway and stopped abruptly, gazing at each other. Zach didn't hug her or make any effort to touch her.

"How are you holding up?" he asked.

"Fine," she answered. "How about you?"

"I'll live." He glanced over at the activity near the rose garden and sighed. "Is there someplace we can talk privately?"

"Sure." Janine's heart leapt to her throat at the sober manner in which he was studying her. "Is everything all right?"

He reassured her with a quick nod. "Of course."

"I don't think anyone's in the kitchen."

"Good." Hand at her elbow, he guided her toward the house. Her fingers were trembling as she pulled out a chair and sat down at the oak table. As he lowered himself into a chair opposite her, she gripped the edge of the table. His eyes had never seemed darker. "Tomorrow's the day."

He said this as if he expected it to come as a shock to Janine. It didn't—but she understood what he was telling her. Time was closing in on them, and if they wanted to back out, it would have to be now.

"Believe me, I know," she said, and her fingers tightened on the table. "Have you had a change of heart?"

"Have you?"

"No, but then again, I haven't had much time to think."

"I've done nothing *but* think about this wedding," Zach said, raking his hands through his hair.

"And?" she prompted, needing reassurance.

He shrugged. "We may both have been fools to agree to this."

"It all happened so fast," Janine said in a weak voice. "One minute we agreed on the word *cherish*, and the next thing I remember, we were deciding we'd be good for each other."

"Don't forget the kissing part," he added. "As I recall, that had quite a bit to do with this decision."

"If you're having second thoughts, I'd rather you said so now than after the ceremony."

His eyes narrowed fleetingly before he slowly shook his head. "No."

"You're sure?"

He answered her by leaning forward, slipping his hand behind her neck, and kissing her soundly. Tenderly. When they broke apart, they were silent. Not talking, not wanting to.

Janine gazed into his dark warm eyes and suddenly she could hardly breathe.

"This is going to be a real marriage," he said forcefully, as if he were expecting an argument.

She nodded. "I most certainly hope so, Mr. Thomas." And her voice was strong and clear.

LESS THAN TWENTY-FOUR HOURS later, Janine stood at Zach's side, prepared to pledge her life to his. She'd never felt more uncertain—or, at the same time, more confident—of anything she'd ever done.

Zach seemed to understand what she was feeling. His eyes held hers as she repeated the words that would bind them.

When she'd finished, Zach slipped his arm around her waist and drew her close to his side. The pastor smiled down on them, then looked to the fifty or so family friends who had gathered on Anton's lawn and said, "I present to you Mr. and Mrs. Zachary Thomas."

A burst of spontaneous applause followed his words.

Before Janine fully realized what was happening, they were mingling with their guests. One minute she was standing in front of the pastor, trembling but unafraid, and the next she was a wife.

"Janine, Janine." Pam rushed to her side before anyone else. "You look so beautiful," she said softly, and bright tears shone in her eyes.

Janine hugged her young friend. "Thank you, sweetheart."

Pam gazed up at Zach and slowly shook her head. "He sure is handsome."

"I think so, too."

Zach arched his brows, cocked his head toward her and murmured, "You never told me that."

"There's no need for you to get a swelled head."

"My children," Gramps said, rejoining them. He hugged Janine close, and she saw that his eyes were as bright as Pam's. "You've never been more beautiful. I swear you look more like my Anna every year."

It was the highest compliment Gramps could have paid her. From the pictures Gramps kept of his wife, Janine knew her grandmother had been exceptionally beautiful.

"Thank you," she said, and lovingly kissed his cheek.

"I have something for you," Pam insisted, thrusting a neatly wrapped box into Janine's hands. "I made them myself," she announced proudly. "I think Zach will like them, too."

"Oh, Pam, you shouldn't have," Janine murmured. Sitting down on the cushioned folding chair, she peeled away the paper and lifted the lid. The moment she did, her breath jammed in her throat. Inside were the sheerest white baby-doll pajamas Janine had ever seen. Her smile faltered as she glanced up to find several people staring at her.

Zach's hand, resting at the nape of Janine's neck, tightened as he spoke, though his voice was warm and amused. "You're right, Pam. I like them very much."

CHAPTER EIGHT

JANINE SAT NEXT to Zach in the front seat of his car. Dressed in a pink suit and matching broad-brimmed hat, she clutched her small floral bouquet. Although the entire wedding had been arranged in seven short days, it had been a lovely affair.

Zach had taken care of planning the short honeymoon trip. All he could spare was three days, so instead of scheduling anything elaborate, he'd suggested they go to his summer place in Ocean Shores, a coastal town two and a half hours by car from Seattle. Janine had willingly agreed.

"So you think I'm handsome," Zach said, keeping his eyes on the road. Neither of them had said much since they'd set off.

"I knew if I said anything it'd go straight to your head, and obviously I was right," she answered. Then, unable to hold back a wide yawn, she pressed the back of her hand to her mouth.

"You're exhausted."

"Are you always this astute?"

"Testy, too."

"I don't mean to be," she apologized. She'd been up before five that morning and in fact, hadn't slept well the entire week. This wasn't exactly the ideal way to start a marriage, and definitely not a honeymoon. There was an added stress, too, that had to do with the honeymoon. Zach had made it understood that he intended their marriage to be a real one, but surely he didn't expect them to share a bed so soon. Or did he?

Every now and again as they drove, she glanced in his direction, wondering what she should say, if anything. Even if she did decide to broach this delicate subject, she wasn't sure how.

"Go ahead and rest," Zach suggested. "I'll wake you when we arrive."

"It shouldn't be too much longer now, should it?"

"Another fifteen minutes or so."

"Then I'll stay awake." Nervously, she twisted the small floral bouquet. Unwrapping Pam's gift had made her all the more apprehensive, but delaying the subject any longer was impossible.

"Zach...are we going to...you know..." she stammered feeling like a complete fool.

"If you're referring to what I think you're referring to, the answer is no. So relax."

"No?" He didn't need to sound so casually certain about it, as if the idea was neither here nor there.

"Why do you ask? Are you having second thoughts about...that?"

"No. Just some reservations."

"Don't worry. When it happens, it happens. The last thing we need to do is pressure one another."

"You're right," she answered, relieved.

"All we need is some time to become comfortable. There's no reason to rush into the physical aspect of our marriage, is there?"

"None whatsoever," she agreed quickly, perhaps too quickly, because when she glanced at him again, Zach was frowning. Yet he seemed so willing to wait, as though their lovemaking was of minor importance. As he'd said, this marriage wasn't one of grand passion. Well, that much was certainly true.

Before another five minutes had passed, Zach left the highway and drove into the resort town of Ocean Shores. He didn't stop in the business district, but headed directly down a side street toward the ocean front. The sun was setting as he pulled into a driveway and turned off the engine.

Janine was too enthralled with the house to say a word.

The wind whipped at them ferociously when they climbed out of the car. Janine held onto her hat with one hand, still clutching the flowers, and to Zach with the other. The sun cast a pink and gold reflection over the rolling hills of sand.

"Home, sweet home," Zach said, nudging her toward the house.

The front door opened before they reached it and a trim middle-aged man stepped onto the porch to greet them. He was grinning broadly. "Hello, Zach. I trust you had a safe trip."

"We did."

"Everything's ready. The cupboards are stocked. The firewood's stacked against the side of the house, and dinner's all prepared."

"Wonderful, Harry, thanks." Zach placed his hand on Janine's shoulder. "This is my wife, Janine," he said, and hesitated. "We were married this afternoon."

"Your wife?" Harry repeated, looking more than a little surprised. "Why that's fantastic. Congratulations to you both."

"Thank you," Janine answered politely.

"Harry Gleason looks after the place for me when I'm not around."

"I'm pleased to meet you, Harry."

"So Zach got himself a wife," Harry said, rubbing the side of his jaw in apparent disbelief. "I couldn't be more—"

"Pleased," a frowning Zach supplied for him, ushering Janine toward the front door.

"Right," Harry said. "I couldn't be more pleased."

Still holding on to her hat, Janine tilted back her head to look over the modern and sprawling single-story house.

"Go on inside," Zach instructed. "I'll get the luggage."

Janine started to protest, suddenly wanting him to follow the traditional wedding custom of carrying her over the threshold. She paused, and Zach gave her a puzzled frown. "Is something wrong?"

"No." She had no real grounds for complaint. She wasn't even sure why it mattered. Swallowing her disappointment, she made her way into the house. She stopped just inside the front door and gazed with wide-eyed wonder at the immense living room with its three long sofas and several upholstered chairs. A brick fireplace took up an entire wall; another was dominated by a floor-to-ceiling window that looked out over the ocean. Drawn to it, Janine watched the waves crash against the shore with a mighty force, as though to punish the sand for some imagined wrong.

Zach followed her inside, carrying their luggage, barely taking time to appreciate the scene before him. "Harry's putting the car away," he said.

"This place is incredible," Janine breathed, gesturing around her. She removed her hat and placed it next to the flowers on the coffee table. She trailed after Zach, and discovered a hallway off which were four bedrooms with an equal number of baths. At the back of the house, she found an exercise room, an office, and an ultramodern kitchen where a pot of coq au vin was simmering on the burner.

In the formal dining room, the long polished mahogany table was set for two. On the deck, designed to take advantage of the ocean view, she found a steaming hot tub along with a bottle of French champagne on ice.

Zach returned as she wandered back into the kitchen and a strained silence fell between them. He was the first to speak. "I put your suitcases in the master bedroom," he said brusquely, shoving his hands into his pockets. "I'm in the one across the hall."

She nodded, not taking time to question her growing sense of disappointment. They'd agreed to delay their wedding night, hadn't they?

"Are you hungry?" he asked, walking to the stove, and lifting the pot's lid, as she had done earlier.

"Only a little. I was thinking about slipping into the hot tub, unless you want to eat first."

"Sure. The hot tub's fine. Whatever you want."

Janine unpacked and located her swimsuit, then changed into it quickly. The warm water sounded appealing. And maybe it would help her relax. Draping a thick beach towel over her arm, she returned to the kitchen, but Zach was nowhere to be seen. Not waiting for him, she walked out to the deck and gingerly stepped into the hot tub. The water felt like a soothing liquid blanket and she slid down, letting it lap just under her breasts.

Zach sauntered onto the deck a minute later, still dressed in his suit. He stopped short when he saw her. "I...didn't realize you'd be out so soon," he said, staring at her with undisguised appreciation. He inhaled sharply and occupied himself by uncorking the bottle of champagne, then pouring himself a liberal glass. He gulped it down, then reached for a second one and filled it for Janine. "You're coming in, aren't you?" she asked, when he handed her the crystal flute.

"Actually, no," he said abruptly. "I won't join you, after all. There were several things I wasn't able to finish at the office this week, and I thought I'd look over some papers. You go ahead and enjoy yourself."

He was going to *work* on their wedding night! But she didn't feel she had any right to comment or complain. She was determined to conceal her bitter disappointment.

"The water's wonderful," she said, as cheerfully as she could manage, hoping her words would convince him to join her.

Zach nodded, but his eyes now avoided Janine. "It looks...great." He strode to the end of the deck, raked his fingers through his hair, then twisted around to face her. He seemed about to say something, but apparently changed his mind.

Baffled by his odd behavior, Janine set aside the glass of champagne and stood up so abruptly that water sloshed over the edges of the tub. "You don't need to say it," she muttered, climbing out and grabbing her towel.

"Say what?"

"You warned me before the wedding, so I walked into this with my eyes wide open. Well, you needn't worry. I got the message the minute we arrived at the house.''

Zach again downed his champagne as though it were water. ''What the hell are you talking about?''

''Never mind.'' Vigorously, she rubbed her arms with the towel.

''No,'' he barked impatiently, ''I want you to tell me.''

Against her better judgment, she pointed a quaking finger toward the front door. ''You went out of your way to tell me how *fond* of me you were and how there wasn't going to be any grand passion. Great. Fine. Perfect. I agreed to those terms. That's all dandy with me, but—''

''But what?'' he demanded.

She squared her shoulders, anticipating an argument. ''But every bride should at least be carried over the threshold.''

''The threshold?'' he cried, looking at her as if she were a prime candidate for intensive counseling. He took two steps away from her and then abruptly turned around. ''You're joking, aren't you?''

She cocked her chin defiantly, refusing to meet his dark eyes. With a lump the size of a watermelon blocking her throat, she dared not try to answer him.

''You're serious. You're actually serious about this!'' He sounded utterly astonished. ''If it's so important to you, then I'll be more than happy to oblige.''

Tears were burning for release, but by sheer force of will, Janine managed to hold them at bay. ''You're the last man on this earth I'd ever allow to carry me anywhere. I'd rather throw myself over this deck than let you touch me.''

"Oh, great, we're fighting. I suppose you're going to ask for a divorce and make this the shortest marriage in Washington history."

Janine paled. Divorce was such an ugly word, and it struck her as hard and viciously as a slap across the face. Despite her efforts, scalding tears brimmed and spilled down her cheeks. With as much dignity as she could muster, which admittedly wasn't much, Janine turned and walked back into the house, leaving a wet trail in her wake.

"Janine," Zach shouted, following her into the kitchen. He hurried ahead of her and planted himself in the doorway, blocking her exit. "Damn it, Janine, arguing with you was the last thing I intended."

With her head held high, she stared past him to a painting of yellow flowers on the dining-room wall. When the tears in her eyes blurred the flowers beyond recognition, she defiantly rubbed the moisture away.

"I'm sorry," he whispered, reaching for her as if he needed to hold her, to touch her. But then his arms fell abruptly to his sides. "I should have realized the wedding traditions would be important to you. To be honest, I completely forgot about the threshold business."

"It's not just that, it's everything. The determined effort to bury yourself in your work. How many other men bring a briefcase with them on their honeymoon? I feel like excess baggage in your life—and we haven't even been married twenty-four hours." She didn't want Zach to swoon at her feet, overcome with passion, but she hadn't expected him to make her feel about as desirable as a load of dirty laundry, either.

Zach looked perplexed. "What does my catching up on reading have to do with any of this?"

His question only irritated her more. "You don't have the foggiest notion of how impossible you are, do you?"

He didn't answer her right away, but seemed to be studying her, weighing his answer before he spoke. "I just thought I might have time to read over some papers," he said slowly. "Apparently that bothers you."

Janine placed her hands on her hips. "Yes, it bothers me."

Zach frowned. "Since we've already agreed to delay the honeymoon part, what would you suggest we do for the next few days?"

"Do you think maybe we could spend the time having fun? Becoming better acquainted?"

"I guess I do seem like a stranger to you," he allowed. "No wonder you're so nervous."

"I am *not* nervous. Just tired and trying hard not to say or do anything that will make you think of me as a...a nag."

"A nag?" Zach repeated incredulously. "I don't think of you as anything but lovely. The truth is, I'm having one heck of a time keeping my eyes off you."

"You are?" The towel she was holding slipped unnoticed to the floor. "I thought you said you didn't know how to say anything romantic."

"That was romantic?"

"And very sweet. I was beginning to think you didn't find me...attractive."

Astonished, Zach stared at her. "You've got to be kidding!"

"I'm not."

"I can see that the next few days are going to be difficult," he said. "You'll just need to be patient with me, all right?"

"All right," she agreed, already feeling worlds better.

"How about if I dish up dinner while you're changing?"

"Great."

By the time she arrived back in the kitchen, wearing warm charcoal slacks and a sweater that was the color of fresh cream, Zach had prepared their meal and poured the wine. He stood behind her chair, politely waiting for her.

"Before we sit down there's something I need to do."

The last thing Janine expected was to be lifted in his strong arms. A gasp of surprise lodged in her throat as her startled gaze flew to his.

"What are you doing?"

"I thought you said you wanted to be carried over the threshold."

"Yes, but you're doing it all wrong. You're supposed to carry me from the outside in—not the other way around."

Zach shrugged, unconcerned. "There's nothing traditional about this marriage. Why start now?" He made a show of pretending his knees were buckling under her weight as he staggered through the living room.

"This is supposed to be serious," she chastised him, but no matter how hard she tried, she couldn't keep the laughter out of her voice.

With a good deal of feigned effort, he managed to open the front door and then ceremoniously step onto the porch. Slowly he released her, letting her feet drop first, holding her upper body close against his chest for a long moment. The humor left his eyes. "There," he said tenderly. "Am I forgetting anything?"

It wouldn't hurt to kiss me, Janine told him in her heart, but the words didn't make it to her lips. When Zach kissed her again, she wanted it to be *his* idea.

"Janine?"

"Everything's perfect. Thank you."

"Not quite," he muttered. He turned her to face him, then covered her mouth with his own. Janine trembled, slipping her arms around his neck and giving herself completely to the kiss. She quivered at the heat that began to warm her from the inside out. This kiss was better than any they'd ever shared, and she hadn't thought that possible. And what that meant, she had no idea.

Zach lifted his mouth abruptly from hers, but his eyes remained closed. Almost visibly he pulled himself together, and when he broke away he seemed completely in control of himself again. Janine sighed inwardly, unsure of what she'd expected.

THE NEXT TWO DAYS flew past. They took long walks on the shore, collecting shells. They rented mopeds and raced along the beach. They launched kites into the sky and delighted in their colorful dipping and soaring. The day before they were scheduled to return to Seattle, Zach declared that he intended to cook dinner. Following that announcement, he informed her he had to go into town to buy the necessary groceries. After the first night, he'd given Harry a week off, and Janine had been fixing simple meals for them.

"What are you serving?" she wanted to know when he pulled into the parking lot of the town's only grocery store. "At least tell me that so I can buy an appropriate wine."

"Wine," he muttered under his breath. "I don't normally serve wine with this dish."

She followed him in, but when he discovered her traipsing down the aisle after him, he gripped her by the shoulders and directed her back outside. "I am an artist, and I insist upon working alone."

Janine had a difficult time not laughing outright.

"In order to make this dinner as perfect as possible, I must concentrate completely on the selection of ingredients. You, my dear sweet wife," he said, pressing his index finger to the tip of her nose, "are too much of a distraction. A lovely one, but nevertheless a distraction."

Janine smiled, her heart singing. Zach was not free with his compliments, and she found herself prizing each one.

While Zach was busy in the grocery store, Janine wandered around town. She bought a lifelike ceramic sea gull, which she promptly named Chester, and a bag of saltwater taffy. Then on impulse, she purchased a bottle of lotion in case they decided to lie out in the sun, tempting a tan.

By the time she returned to the car, Zach was waiting for her. She was licking a double-decker chocolate ice-cream cone and feeling incredibly happy.

"Did the master chef find everything he needed?" she asked. Two brown paper bags were sitting on the floor and she restrained herself from peeking inside.

"Our meal tonight will be one you'll long remember, I promise you."

"I'm glad to hear it." Holding out her ice-cream cone, she asked. "Do you want a taste?"

"Please." He rejected the offer of the cone itself and instead bent forward and lowered his mouth to hers. As she gazed into his dark heavy-lidded eyes her heart accelerated and she was filled with a sudden intense longing. Janine wasn't sure what was happening between them, but it felt, quite simply, right.

Although the kiss was fleeting, a shiver of awareness twisted its way down her back. Neither of them spoke or moved. He'd meant the kiss to be gentle and teasing, but it had quickly found another purpose. For a breathless second, the smile faded from his eyes. He continued to hold her, and his breathing was rapid and hard.

After nearly two full days alone together, Janine found it amusing that when he finally chose to kiss her, he'd do it in a crowded parking lot.

"I don't remember chocolate being quite that rich," he murmured. He strove for a casual tone, but Janine wasn't fooled. He was as affected by the kiss as she, and struggling just as hard to disguise it.

They were both uncharacteristically quiet on the short drive back to the house. Until the kiss, they'd spent companionable days together, enjoying one another's company. Then, in the space of no more than a couple of seconds, all that had changed.

"Am I banished from the kitchen?" Janine asked once they were inside the house, forcing an airy note into her voice.

"Not entirely," Zach surprised her by saying. "I'll need you later to wash the dishes."

Janine laughed and pulled her suntan lotion out of her bag. While Zach puttered around inside, she changed into her swimsuit, then dragged the lounge chair into the sun to soak up the last of the afternoon's rays.

Zach soon joined her, carrying a tall glass of iced tea. "You look like you could use this."

"Thanks. If I'd known how handy you were in the kitchen, I'd have let you assume the duties long before now."

He set the glass down beside her and headed back to the kitchen. "You'd be amazed at the list of my talents," he threw over his shoulder.

Kissing was certainly one of them, she thought. The sample he'd given her earlier had created a sharp unexpected need for more. If she was a sophisticated experienced kind of woman, she wouldn't have any problem working her way back into his arms. It would all appear so effortless and casual. He'd kiss her, and she'd kiss him back, and before either of them realized what was happening, they'd truly be husband and wife.

Lying on her back with her eyes closed, Janine imagined how wonderful it would be if Zach were to take her in his arms and make love to her. . . .

She awoke from her doze with a start. She hurried inside to change, and by the time she was finished, Zach announced that dinner was ready to be served. He'd set the patio table so they could eat on the deck.

"Do you need any help?" she asked, trying to peek inside the kitchen.

"None. Sit down before everything cools." He pointed to the chair and waited until she was comfortable.

"I only have a spoon," she said, after unfolding the napkin on her lap. He must have made a mistake.

"A spoon is all you'll need," he shouted to her from inside the kitchen.

Playfully she asked, "You went to all this trouble for soup?"

"Wait and see. I'll be there in a minute."

He sounded so serious, Janine couldn't keep from smiling. She was running through a list of words to praise his efforts—"deliciously unique," "refreshingly different"—when Zach walked onto the deck, carrying a tin can with a pair of tongs.

"Good grief, what's that?" she asked in dismay.

"Dinner," he said. "The only real cooking I ever did was while I belonged to the Boy Scouts."

As though he was presenting lobster bisque, he set the steaming can in front of her. Janine leaned forward, almost afraid to view its contents.

"Barbecue beans. With sliced hot dogs," he announced proudly.

"And to think I doubted you."

Her reservations vanished, however, the moment she tasted his specialty. The beans were actually very good. He surprised her, too, by bringing out dessert, a concoction consisting of graham crackers covered with melted chocolate and marshmallows. He'd warmed them in the oven and served them on a cookie sheet.

Janine ate four of what Zach called "some-mores." He explained that once they'd been tasted, everyone asked for "some more."

"I don't know how you've managed to stay single all these years," she teased, forgetting for the moment that they were married. "If the news about your talent in the kitchen got out, women would be knocking down your door."

Zach chuckled, looking extraordinarily pleased with himself.

An unexpected thought entered Janine's mind, filling her with curiosity. It astonished her now that she'd never asked Zach about other women in his life. It would be naive to assume he'd never had involvements. She'd had her relationship with Brian; surely there were women in Zach's past.

She waited until later that night when they were sipping wine and listening to classical music in front of the fireplace. Zach seemed relaxed, sitting with one knee raised and the other leg stretched in front of him. Janine lay on her stomach, staring into the fire.

"Have you ever been in love?" She was striving for a casual tone.

Zach didn't answer her right away. "Would you be jealous if I said I had?"

"No." She sounded more confident than she felt.

"I thought not. What about you?"

She took her time answering, too. She'd thought she was in love with Brian. It wasn't until later, after the pain of Brian's rejection had eased, that she realized she'd been in love with the *idea* of being in love.

"No," she said, feeling completely honest in her response. What she felt for Zach, whom she was only beginning to know, was already a thousand times stronger than anything she'd ever felt for a man. She didn't know how to explain it, so she avoided the issue by reminding him, "I asked you first."

"I'm a married man. Naturally I'm in love."

"You're fond of me, remember?"

"I thought you detested that word."

"I do. Now stop tiptoeing around the subject. Have you ever really been in love—I mean head over heels in love? You don't need to go into any detail—a simple yes or no will suffice."

"A desperate-passion kind of being in love?"

"Yes," she told him, growing impatient. "Don't make fun of me and please don't give me a list of all the women you've been *fond* of."

He grew so quiet and so intense that her smile began to fade. She pulled herself into a sitting position and looped her arms around her bent knees.

Zach stared at her for a long moment. As she watched the harsh pain move into his eyes, Janine felt her chest tighten.

"Yes," he answered in a hoarse whisper. "I've been in love."

CHAPTER NINE

"HER NAME was Marie."

"Marie," Janine repeated the name as though she'd never heard it before.

"We met in Europe when I was on assignment with the armed services. She spoke five languages fluently and helped me learn my way around two of them in the time we worked together."

"She was in the service with you?"

"I was army, she worked for the secret service. We were thrown together for a top-secret project that was only supposed to last a few days and instead dragged on for weeks."

"This was when you fell in love with her?" The ache inside her chest wouldn't go away. Her heart felt weighted down with the pain.

"We both were aware the assignment was a dangerous one, and our working closely together was essential." He paused, sighing deeply. "To make a long story short, I fell in love with her. But she didn't love me."

"And then what?"

"I wanted her to leave the service and marry me. She wasn't interested. If you insist on knowing the details, I'll give them to you."

"No."

Zach took a sip of his wine. "I left the army shortly after that. I didn't have the heart for it anymore. Unlike Marie—her work, with all its risks, was her whole life. She was the most dedicated and bravest woman I've ever known. Although it was painful at the time, she was right to reject my proposal. Marriage and a family would have bored her within a year. It was painful, don't misunderstand me. I loved her more than I thought it possible to care for another human being."

They both were silent for a moment, then Janine asked, "What did you do once you left the army?"

"Over the years, I'd managed to put aside some money, make a few investments. Once I was on my own, I decided to go into business for myself. I read everything I could get my hands on about the business-supply field and modeled the way I dealt with my clients and accounts after your grandfather's enterprise. Within five years, I was his major competitor. We met at a conference last year, and decided that instead of competing against each other, we'd join forces. And as they say, the rest is history."

"Was she pretty?" Even as she asked the question, Janine knew it was ridiculous. What possible difference would it make if his Marie was a former Miss America or had a face like a gorilla? None. Zach had loved Marie. Loved her as he would probably never love again. Loved her more than he'd thought it was possible to love another human being. By comparison, what he felt for her, Janine, was indeed only fondness.

"She was blond and, yes, she was beautiful."

Janine made a feeble attempt at a smile. "Somehow I knew that."

Zach shook himself lightly as if dragging himself back to the present and away from the powerful lure of the past. "You don't need to worry. It was a long time ago."

"I wasn't worried," Janine muttered. She got to her feet and collected their wineglasses. "I'm a little tired. If you don't mind I think I'll go to bed now."

Zach was still staring into the fire and Janine doubted that he'd even heard her. She didn't need a crystal ball to realize he was thinking of the beautiful Marie.

No more than ten minutes after she'd turned out her bedroom light, Janine heard Zach move down the hallway to his room. It sounded for a moment as if he'd hesitated in front of her door, but Janine convinced herself that was just wishful thinking.

From the moment Zach had told her about the one great love of his life, Janine had felt as if a lump were building inside her. A huge lump of disillusionment that seemed to be located somewhere between her heart and her stomach. With every breath she took, it grew larger. Good grief, why should she care about Marie? Zach had never confessed to any deep feeling for her. He hadn't cheated her out of anything that was her right.

An hour later, she lay on her side, still wide awake, her hands pressed to her stomach. She didn't mind that Zach had loved another woman so deeply, but what did hurt was that he could never love her with the same intensity. Marrying her, he'd claimed, made practical and financial sense. He was *fond* of her.

Like a romantic idiot, Janine had been frolicking through their short marriage, confident they would soon be in love with each other and live happily ever after with their two-point-five children in their happy little home with the white picket fence.

Zach had loved Marie, who'd dedicated herself to serving her country.

The most patriotic thing Janine had ever done was cast her vote at election time. She didn't think she should include the two occasions she'd made coffee at Red Cross meetings.

Marie was a linguist. After two years of high-school French, Janine was a master at conjugating verbs, but hopelessly lost in real conversation.

"I had to ask," she groaned to herself. She was fairly confident that Zach would never have mentioned Marie if she hadn't forced the subject. How blissful her ignorance had been. How comfortable.

She could never be the great love of his life and would always remain in the background. Far in the background...

When Janine heard Zach moving around the house a few hours later, she rolled over and glanced at the clock, sure it was still the middle of the night. Then she noticed it was midmorning; they'd planned to be on the road before now. Tossing aside the blankets, she stumbled out of bed and reached blindly for her robe. But she wasn't paying attention, because she collided with the wall and gave a loud shout of pain. She cupped her hand over her nose and closed her eyes. Tears rolled slowly down her cheeks.

"Janine." Zach pounded on the door. "Are you all right?"

"No," she cried, still holding her nose. She glanced in the mirror and lowered her hand. Just as she'd suspected, her nose was bleeding.

"Can I come in?" Zach asked next.

"No...go away." She headed for the adjoining bathroom, tilting back her head as far as she could and pressing both hands over her nose.

"You sound funny. I'm coming in."

"No," she hollered again, "Go away." She groped for a washcloth. The tears rained down now, more from humiliation than pain.

"I'm coming in," Zach shouted, sounding distinctly irritated.

Before Janine could protest, the bedroom door flew open and Zach stalked inside. He stopped abruptly in the bathroom doorway. "What happened?"

Pressing the cold cloth over the lower half of her face with one hand, Janine gestured violently with the other, demanding that he leave.

"Let me look at that," he said, obviously determined to deal with her bloody nose, as well as her anger. He pushed gently against her shoulders, lowering her onto the edge of the bathtub, and carefully removed the cloth.

"What did you do? Meet up with a prize fighter?"

"Don't you dare make fun of me!" The tears ran down her cheeks again and plummeted like raindrops against her silk collar.

It took only a minute or so to control the bleeding. Zach seemed to know exactly what to do. Janine no longer had any desire to fight, and she allowed him to do what he wanted.

Gently, Zach brushed the tears from her cheeks. "Do you want me to kiss it and make it better?"

Without waiting for an answer, Zach's mouth captured hers. Janine felt herself go completely and utterly still. Her heart started to explode and before she realized what she was doing, she'd linked her arms around his neck and was clinging to him helplessly. Zach kissed her forehead and her eyes. His thumbs brushed the remaining moisture from her cheeks. Then he nuzzled her neck. Trembling, she immersed herself in his tenderness. No matter what had happened in the past, Zach was hers for this minute, for this day.

Zach lifted Janine to her feet and seemed to be leading her toward the bed. She might have been tempted to let him, if she hadn't learned about his love for Marie. Knowing she would always place a distant second in his affections was a crippling blow to her pride—and to her heart. It would take time and effort to accept that she could never be the woman who evoked an all-consuming passion in him.

With that thought in mind, she gently pushed him away, needing to put some distance between them before it was too late.

Accepting Janine's decision, Zach dropped his arms and moved to lean against the doorjamb, as if he needed its support to remain upright.

Janine couldn't look at him, couldn't speak. She turned away and began fumbling with her clothes.

"I'll give you a few minutes to dress while I start loading up the car," Zach said a moment later, sounding oddly unlike himself.

Janine nodded miserably. There was nothing she could say. Nothing she could do. He'd wanted to make love to her, and she'd turned him away.

While he packed the car, Janine dressed. She met him fifteen minutes later, her suitcase in hand. She was determined to be cool. But not too cool. Friendly, she decided, but not excessively friendly.

"I'm ready," she announced, with her most cheerful smile.

Zach locked up the house, and in a few moments they were on their way. Deciding to pretend there was nothing out of the ordinary, Janine chatted amicably during the drive home. If Zach noticed anything was wrong, he didn't comment. For his part, he seemed as hesitant as she to talk about what had happened. They seemed to be of one mind about the morning's incident. The whole thing was best forgotten.

Only once did Zach refer to it. He asked her if her nose was causing her any pain, but she quickly assured him she was fine. She flashed a smile bright enough to blind him and immediately changed the subject.

The Seattle sky was gray and drizzling rain when they pulled into the parking garage at the downtown condominium owned by Zach. Silently, she helped him unload the car. They were both unusually quiet as they rode the elevator to the tenth floor.

Zach paused outside his door and eyed her skeptically. "Am I obligated to haul you over the threshold again, or is once enough?"

"Once is enough."

"Good." He grinned and unlocked the door, then pushed it open for her to precede him. Curious, she quickened her pace as she walked inside. The living room was a warm mixture of leather and wood, and its wide window offered a breathtaking view of the Seattle skyline.

"It's lovely."

He nodded, seeming pleased at her reaction. "If you don't like it, we can move. I suppose now that we're married, we should think about purchasing a house soon.''

"Why?" she inquired innocently.

"I'm hoping we'll have children someday. Whenever you're ready, that is. There's no pressure, Janine.''

"I . . . know that." She looked past him at the panoramic view, and wrapped her arms around her middle, her heart reacting immediately to his words.

Walking to his desk, Zach pushed the "play" button on his answering machine. A long stream of apparently business-related messages followed.

Janine was much too interested in exploring the condominium to stand and listen to three days' worth of communications. She wandered from room to room, eager to see her new home. In the hallway, she noted Zach had diplomatically left her luggage on the carpet outside the two bedrooms. His was in the master. In his own way, he was telling her that where she slept would be her own decision. If she wished to become his wife in the fullest sense, all she had to do was place her suitcase in the master bedroom. Nothing more needed to be said.

It didn't take Janine longer than a second to decide. She lifted her suitcase and headed toward the guest bedroom. When she looked up, Zach was standing in the hall, studying her, his expression pained.

"Unless you need me for anything, I'm going to the office," he said gruffly.

"That'll be fine."

His gaze moved past her and rested meaningfully on the mattress in the guest bedroom. He cocked one eyebrow questioningly as though to offer her the opportunity to reconsider. "Are you sure you'd rather sleep in here?" he asked.

"I'm sure."

Zach dragged his fingers through his hair. "I was afraid of that."

A minute later, he was gone.

ZACH DIDN'T COME HOME for dinner that night. Janine had been in the bathroom when the phone rang, and Zach had left her a message on the machine that he'd be late. So she ate by herself in front of the television, feeling abandoned and unloved. She was just putting the dishes into the dishwasher when he arrived home.

"Sorry I'm late."

"No problem," she lied, never having felt more alone.

Zach glanced through the mail on his desk, although Janine was sure he'd looked at it earlier. "You got the message I wouldn't be home for dinner?"

"Yes. Did you want anything to eat? I could fix you something."

"I ate earlier. Thanks anyway."

They watched an hour's worth of television and then decided to go to bed.

Janine changed into her pajamas—the same no-nonsense type she'd been wearing all week, for she couldn't bring herself to wear the dainty baby-dolls that Pam had given her—and had just finished washing her face. She was coming out of the bathroom, her toothbrush clenched between her teeth, when she nearly collided with Zach in the hallway. She'd forgotten her slippers and was going to her bedroom to retrieve them. They'd already said their good-nights, and Janine hadn't expected to see him again until morning. She wasn't prepared for this encounter, and the air between them was thick with tension.

She had to force herself not to carelessly toss her toothbrush aside. Not to tell him how she longed for him to love her with the same intensity he had with Marie.

His hands reached out to steady her, and when she didn't immediately move away, he ran the tips of his fingers down her thick brown hair, edging her long bangs to the side of her face so he could gaze into her blue eyes.

Janine lowered her head and closed her eyes. "Eshbloo me," she managed, but it was difficult to speak with a toothbrush poking out of her mouth.

"Pardon?"

Janine hurried back to the bathroom and rinsed out her mouth. Turning, she braced her hands against the edge of the sink. "I said excuse me for bumping into you."

"Will you be comfortable in the guest room?"

"Yes, fine."

He held a thick blanket in his arms. "I thought you might need this."

"Thanks," she said as smoothly as possible, coming out of the bathroom to take the blanket from him. She longed to be swept off her feet. She wanted love. She wanted passion.

He was offering a warm blanket.

"I...phoned Gramps," she said, looking for a way to delay their parting, and cursing herself for her weakness.

"I intended to get hold of him myself, but got sidetracked."

"He sounded chipper. Dr. Coleman and a couple of his other friends were at the house and the four of them were playing pinochle."

"I'm pleased to hear he's enjoying his retirement."

"I am, too."

A short silence followed.

"Good night, Janine," Zach said after a moment. He glanced, frowning, into the guest room.

"Good night," she said awkwardly.

Janine was certain neither of them slept a wink that night. They were across the hall from each other, but they might as well have been on opposite sides of the state, so great was the emotional distance between them.

In the morning, when Zach's alarm rang, Janine was already wide awake. She threw back her covers, dressed and had coffee waiting when he entered the kitchen.

Zach seemed surprised to see her. "Thanks," he murmured, when she handed him a cup. "That's a very... wifely thing to do."

"What? Make coffee?"

"Get up to see your husband off to work."

"I happened to be awake and figured I might as well get out of bed."

He opened the refrigerator, reached for the orange juice and poured himself a glass. "I see." He replaced the carton and leaned against the counter. "You did agree that our marriage would be a real one."

"Yes, I did," she said somewhat defensively. But that agreement had been before she'd learned about the one great love of his life. Zach had warned her their marriage would be advantageous for a variety of reasons, the least of which was love. At the time, Janine had willingly agreed, convinced their relationship would find a storybook ending. One day they'd gaze at each other and realize they were madly in love. Now she understood that would never happen. And she didn't know if she could stand it.

"Janine," Zach said, distracting her, "is something wrong?"

"What could possibly be wrong?"

"Obviously something's bothering you. You look like you've lost your best friend."

"You should have told me," she burst out, running from the kitchen.

"Told you what?" Zach shouted, following her down the hall.

Furious, she hurried into her bedroom and sat on the end of the mattress, her hands clenched into tight fists at her sides.

"What are you talking about?" he demanded, blocking the doorway.

"About . . . this other woman you loved."

"Marie? What about her? What's she got to do with you and me?"

"You said you lost your heart when she rejected you. You loved her . . . She was brave and wonderful, and I'm not any of those things. I don't take pain very well and . . . I'd like to be patriotic but all I do is vote and all I know in French are verbs."

"What's any of that got to do with you and me?" Zach repeated hoarsely, then tossed his hands into the air. "What the hell has that got to do with anything?"

Knowing she'd never be able to explain, Janine shook her head, sending her bangs fanning out in several directions. "All you are is *fond* of me."

"Correction," Zach said as he stepped into the bedroom. "I *cherish* you."

"It isn't enough," she said, feeling miserable and wretched and unworthy.

"What do you mean it isn't enough? According to you the only reason you married me was that I was a good kisser, so you can't fault me for *my* reasons."

"I don't, it's just that you...you never told me about loving someone else, and if loving her wasn't bad enough, she was a hero, too. All you feel for me is fondness. Well, I don't want your fondness, Zachary Thomas," she cried, leaping to her feet. She tried to collect her scattered thoughts. "If you cared for me, then you would have told me about Marie before. Not mentioning her was a form of dishonesty. You were completely...unfair."

Zach's expression darkened and he buried his hands in his pockets. "You, my dear, didn't say one word to me about Brian."

Janine was so shocked she sank back into the bed. Zach still glared at her, challenging her to contradict him. Slowly gathering her composure, she stood, her eyes narrowing as she studied her husband. "Who told you about Brian?"

"Your grandfather."

"How did he know? I never said a word to him about Brian. Not one solitary word."

"Obviously he knew."

"Obviously." Janine had never felt more like weeping. "I suppose he told you that Brian lied to me and claimed to love me when all the while he was seeing another girl on the side." Another, more troubling thought entered her mind. "I...bet Gramps used the story to make you feel sorry for me, sorry enough to agree to marry me."

"Janine, no."

She covered her face with both hands, humiliation burning her cheeks. It was all so much worse than she'd ever imagined. "You felt sorry for me, didn't you?"

Zach paced the length of the bedroom. "I'm not going to lie to you, although I have a notion it would be better if I did. Your grandfather didn't mention that you'd fallen in love with Brian until after the day we took him to the doctor."

"He waited until we got to know each other a little better," Janine whispered, still dealing with the realization that her grandfather had known about Brian all along.

"By then I'd discovered I liked you."

"The word *like* is possibly even worse than *fond*," she muttered.

"Just hear me out, would you?"

"All right," she sighed, fearing that nothing he said now mattered, anyway. Her pride had just suffered another major blow. The one love of his life had been this marvelous patriot, while Janine had fallen for a weak-willed womanizer.

"It isn't as bad as it seems," Zach tried to assure her.

"I can just imagine what Gramps told you."

"All he said was that he was afraid you'd never learn to trust your own judgment again. For quite a while now, he's watched you avoid any hint of a relationship. It was as though you'd retreated from men and were content to just lick your wounds."

"That's not true. I was seeing Peter Donahue on a regular basis."

"Safe dates with safe men. There was never any likelihood of your falling in love with Peter and you knew it. It was the only reason you went out with him."

"Is...is what happened with Brian why Gramps decided to play matchmaker?"

"I suspect that was part of it. Also his concern for your future. But I don't fully understand his intentions even now. I don't think it matters. He wanted you to be happy and secure. Anton knew I'd never purposely hurt you. And in his eyes, the two of us were perfect for each other." Zach sat down next to her and reached for her hand, lacing her fingers with his own. "Does it matter so much? We're married now."

She looked away from him, and swallowed tightly. "I...may not be blond and gorgeous or even brave, but I deserve a husband who'll love me. Both Gramps and you failed to take that into account. I don't want your pity, Zach Thomas."

"Good, because I don't pity you. You're my wife, and frankly, I'm happy about it. We can have a good life, if you'll put this nonsense behind you."

"You'd never have chosen me on your own. I knew what you thought of me from the first moment we met. You thought, you assumed I was a rich spoiled woman who'd never had anything real to worry about. I bet you thought I'd consider a broken nail a major disaster."

"All right, I'll admit I had the wrong impression, but that was before," Zach insisted.

"Before what?"

"Before I got to know you."

Janine's shoulders heaved with barely suppressed emotion. "As I recall you suggested the reason you'd be willing to marry me was because I wasn't so bad. I guess I should have swooned with the sheer thrill of such compliments."

Zach's sigh was filled with frustration. "I told you before I wasn't ever going to say the stuff you women like to hear. I don't know a damn thing about romance. But I care about you, Janine, I honestly care. Isn't that enough?"

"I need more than that," she said miserably. It was the promise of their future, the promise of learning about love together, that had intrigued her.

Zach frowned. "You told me even before we were married that you didn't need romantic words. You were content before I ever mentioned Marie. How has my telling you changed anything?"

She saw that Zach was losing his patience with her. She lowered her gaze to the thick carpet and swallowed hard. "I really wish I could explain, but it does make a difference. I'm sorry, Zach, I really am."

A lifetime seemed to pass before he spoke again. "So am I," he whispered before turning away. A moment later the front door opened and almost immediately closed again. Zach had left her.

"What did you expect?" she wailed, covering her face with both hands. "Did you think he was going to fall at your knees and declare his undying love?" The picture of the proud and mighty Zach Thomas playing the role of besotted husband was almost comical. If he'd done that for any woman it would have been the brave and beautiful Marie. Not Janine.

AFTER THAT DISASTROUS morning, their relationship grew more strained than ever. Zach left for work early and returned late, usually past dinnertime. Janine never questioned where he was or who he was with, although she nearly had to bite off her tongue to keep from asking.

Zach proved to be a model housemate, if not a husband—cordial, courteous and remote. For her part, she threw herself into her volunteer work at the Friendship Club, spending several hours each week with the youngsters. She did her best to hide her unhappiness from her grandfather, although that was difficult.

"You look pale," he told her when she joined him for lunch one afternoon, several days after her return from Ocean Shores. "Are you losing weight?"

"I wish," she said, attempting to make a joke of it. They sat in the dining room, with Mrs. McCormick wandering in and out, casting Janine concerned glances. Janine resisted the urge to leap up and do aerobic exercises to demonstrate that she was in perfect health.

"You can't afford to get much thinner," Gramps said, eyeing her solemnly. He placed a dinner roll on the side of her plate and plunked the butter dish down in front of her.

"I'm not losing weight," she chided, spreading a thick layer of butter on the roll in order to please him.

"I took that sea gull you gave me into the office," Gramps said as he continued to study her. "Zach saw it and asked me where I got it. When I told him, he didn't say anything, but I could tell he wasn't pleased. Do you want it back?"

"No, of course not." Janine dropped her gaze. She'd never intended for Gramps to take Chester into the office. On impulse, she'd given him the ceramic bird, reluctant to have it around the condominium to remind her of those first glorious days with Zach.

"I wish I knew what was wrong with you two," Gramps burst out in an uncharacteristic display of frustration. He tossed his napkin onto his dinner plate. "You should be happy! Instead, the pair of you look like you're recovering from a bad bout of flu. Zach's working so many hours it's a wonder he doesn't fall over from sheer exhaustion."

Janine carefully tore the roll into quarters. She toyed with the idea of bringing up the subject of Brian, but in the end, she didn't.

"So you say you're fine, and there's nothing wrong between you and Zach," Gramps muttered sarcastically. "Funny, that's exactly what he said when I asked him. Only he told me to mind my own business—not quite in those words, but I got the message. The thing is, the boy looks as pathetic as you do. I can't understand it—you're perfect for each other!"

Gramps reached into his pocket for a cigar. "I'll be seeing Zach this afternoon and I fully intend to give that boy a piece of my mind. By all rights, you should be a happy bride." He tapped one end of the cigar against the table.

"We'll be fine, Gramps. Please stay out of it."

For a long moment, he said nothing; he only stared at the cigar between his fingers. "You're sure you don't want me to talk some sense into that boy?" he finally asked.

The mental picture of him trying to do so was enough to bring a quivering smile to her lips. "I'm sure," she said, then glanced at her watch. Pam would be waiting for her. "But since you're seeing Zach, would you mind letting him know I'll probably be late for dinner? He...should go ahead and eat without me."

"Do you do this often?" His question was an accusation.

"No," she replied, shaking her head. "This is the first time. Pam needs my help with a school project and I don't know when we'll be finished."

Gramps glowered as he lit his cigar, puffing mightily before he spoke. "I'll tell him."

AS IT TURNED OUT, Janine spent longer with Pam than she'd expected. The homework assignment wasn't difficult, but Pam begged Janine to stay with her. Pam's father was working late and the girl seemed to need Janine more than ever. They cooked dinner together, then ate in front of the television while Pam chatted away about her friends and life in general.

It was almost nine by the time Janine pulled into the parking garage. The first thing she noticed was Zach's car. The atmosphere had been so terribly falsely courteous between them that she dreaded each encounter, however brief. Since that first morning, Zach hadn't made any effort to talk to her about her role in his life. Janine wasn't looking for a long flowery declaration of love. Just a word or two more profound than *fond* or *like* to let her know she was important to him.

Drawing a deep calming breath, she headed for the condominium.

She'd just unlocked the door when Zach stormed into the room like a Minnesota blizzard. "Just where the hell have you been?" he demanded.

Janine was so shocked by his fierce anger that she said nothing.

"I demand as your husband to know exactly where you were." Zach jammed his fingers viciously through his hair.

She removed her sweater, hanging it carefully in the entryway closet along with her purse. Zach scowled at her silence, fists clenched at his sides. "Do you have any idea of the time? Did it so much as cross your mind that I might have been concerned about you?"

Janine turned to face him. "You knew where I was," she said calmly.

"All Anton said was that you'd be late. Not where you were going or who you were with. So naturally I was worried."

"I'm sorry. Next time I'll leave you Pam's phone number in case you need to contact me." Janine yawned and covered her mouth with both hands. The day had been exhausting. "If you don't mind, I think I'll go to bed now. Unless there's anything else you'd like to know?"

He glared at her, then shook his head, before wheeling around abruptly and walking away.

Hours later, Janine was awakened from a light sleep by a gruff sobbing sound coming from the other room. It didn't take her more than a moment to realize it was Zach. Was he having a nightmare?

Tossing aside the blankets, she hurried out of bed and into his room. The cries of anguish grew louder and more intense. In the light from the hallway, she could see him thrashing about, the bedding in disarray.

"Zach," she cried, rushing to his side. She sat on the edge of the bed and placed her hands gently on his shoulders. "Wake up. You're having a dream. Just a dream. It's okay...."

Zach's eyes slowly opened. "Janine." He ground out her name as though in torment, and reached for her, hauling her into his arms with such force that he left her breathless. "Dear Lord," he said, his voice so husky she could barely understand him. "I thought I'd lost you."

CHAPTER TEN

"ZACH, I'M FINE," Janine whispered. Emotion clogged her throat at the hungry way his eyes roamed her face. He seemed to have difficulty believing, even now, that she was unhurt.

"It was so real," he continued, his chest heaving. He covered his face as if to block out the vivid images the dream had induced. Making room in the large bed, he brought her down beside him. His hands repeatedly stroked her hair from her face as he released several jagged breaths. "We were at the ocean," he told her, "and although I'd warned you against it, you decided to swim. A huge wave knocked you off your feet and you were drowning. Heaven help me, I tried, but I couldn't get to you fast enough." He closed his eyes briefly. "You kept calling out to me and I couldn't find you. I just couldn't get to you fast enough."

"Zach," she whispered, her mouth so close to his that their breath mingled, "I'm right here. It was only a dream. It wasn't real."

He nodded, but his eyes still seemed troubled, refusing to leave her face. Then ever so slowly, as though he expected her to object, he moved his mouth even closer to hers. "I couldn't bear to lose you. I'd rather die myself."

Helpless to deny him anything, Janine turned her face to receive his kiss.

His hands tangled her thick dark hair, effectively holding her captive, while his mouth seized hers in a devouring kiss that sent her senses swirling into a place where nothing mattered except his touch. Overcome for a moment by the fierce tenderness she felt in him, Janine eagerly fed his need.

"Janine, oh, my dear sweet Janine. I couldn't bear to lose you."

"I'm here...I'm here." Melting against him, she molded her body to the unyielding contours of his, offering her lips and her heart to his loving possessiveness. Again and again, he kissed her. Janine slid her hands up his chest and twined them around his neck. This was what she'd longed for from the first, the knowledge that he needed her, and she gloried in the warm sensations.

With a groan, he reluctantly dragged his mouth from hers. He held her clasped firmly to his chest and his breathing was both harsh and rapid. Complete and utter peace combined with a delirious sense of happiness, and she released a deep sigh. Pressing her ear to his muscled chest, she listened, content, to the heavy pounding of his heart.

"Did I frighten you?" he asked after a moment.

"No," she whispered.

He resumed stroking her hair as she nestled more securely in his arms. Zach had made her feel wondrous, exciting things every time he'd kissed her, but the way he held and touched her now went far beyond those kisses. She'd experienced a bonding with Zach, a true joining of spirits that had been missing until now. He had told her he would cherish her, but she hadn't believed it until this moment. Tears clouded her eyes and she struggled to restrain them.

For a long time neither of them spoke. But Janine didn't need words. Her eyes were closed as she savored these precious moments.

When Zach did speak, his voice was little more than a hoarse whisper. "I had a sister who drowned. Her name was Beth Ann, and I promised I'd always be there for her—but I failed her. I couldn't bear to lose you, too."

Janine tightened her hold, knowing how difficult it must be for him to speak of his sister.

"I never forgave myself." His body tensed and his fingers dug roughly into her shoulder. "Losing Beth Ann still haunts me. She wouldn't have drowned if I'd been with her. She—"

Lifting her head slightly, Janine's misty gaze met his. "It wasn't your fault. How could it have been?"

"But I was responsible for her," he returned harshly.

Janine suspected that Zach had rarely, if ever, shared his sorrow or his guilt over his sister's death with anyone. A low groan worked its way through him and he squeezed his eyes tightly shut. "For years, I've drummed out the memories of Beth Ann's death. The nightmare was so real, only this time it wasn't her—it was you."

"But I'm safe and sound. See?" She pressed her hands to both sides of his face, smiling down on him.

He sighed and smiled back, a little uncertainly. "I'm all right now. I shouldn't have burdened you with this."

"It wasn't a burden."

His arms tightened around her, and he inhaled deeply as if soaking in her scent, absorbing her softness. "Stay with me?"

She nodded, satisfied that he needed her.

Within minutes, Janine felt herself drifting into drowsiness. From Zach's relaxed, even breathing, she knew he was already asleep.

When Janine next stirred, she was lying on her side, and Zach was cuddling her spoon fashion, his arm looped about her waist. At some point during the night, she'd slipped under the covers, but she had no recollection of doing so. A small satisfied smile touched the edges of her mouth. She rolled carefully onto her back so as not to disturb Zach, and wondered what she should do. When Zach woke and found her in bed with him, she feared he might regret what had happened, regret asking her to stay. In the harsh light of day, he might feel embarrassed that he'd told her about his sister's death and the guilt he bore.

Closing her eyes, Janine debated with herself. If she slipped from his bed and returned to her own room, he might think she was rejecting him, shocked by his heart-wrenching account of Beth Ann's death.

"Janine?" He whispered her name, his voice still husky with sleep.

Her eyes flew open. "I . . . we fell asleep. What time is it?"

"Early. The alarm won't go off for another couple of hours."

She nodded, hoping to disguise any hint of disappointment in her voice. He didn't want her with him, she was sure of it. He was embarrassed to find her still in his bed. "I'll leave now if you want."

"No."

The single word was filled with such longing that Janine thought she'd misunderstood him. She managed to tip her head back far enough to meet his gaze. The light from the hall allowed her to see the passion smoldering in his rich dark eyes. Turning onto her side so she faced him, Janine lovingly traced the lines of his face.

"I'm sorry about the way I behaved over...Marie," she whispered. "I was jealous and I knew I was being ridiculous, but I couldn't help myself."

The corners of his eyes crinkled with his smile. "I'll forgive you, if you're willing to overlook the way I behaved when you arrived home last night."

She answered him with a light kiss, and he hugged her to him. Janine surrendered to the sheer pleasure of being in Zach's arms, savoring the rush of warm sensations that sprang to life inside her.

"I don't know how to say all the words you deserve to hear, but I know one thing, Janine. I love you. It happened without my even being aware of it. One day I woke up and realized how important you'd become to me. It wasn't the grand passion you wanted, and I'm sorry for that. The love I feel for you is the quiet steady kind. It's buried deep in my heart, but trust me, it's there. You're the most important person in my life."

"Oh, Zach, I love you so much."

"You love me?"

"I have for weeks, even before we were married, I think. That's what bothered me so much when I learned about Marie. I wanted you to love me with the same intensity that you felt for her...that I feel for you."

"It isn't like that. It never was. Marie was as brave as she was beautiful, but what we shared was never meant to last. And she was smart enough to realize it. I fell in love with her, but she was too much of a professional ever to involve her heart. She was the kind of person who thrives on excitement and danger. It wasn't until you and I met that I realized if I were ever to marry, it would be to someone like you."

"Someone like me?"

He kissed her briefly. "A woman who's warm and gentle and caring. Someone unselfish and—" he hesitated "—and desirable."

Her throat tightened with emotion. It was all she could do to meet his gaze. Zach found her desirable. He wanted to make love to her. He didn't need to say the words; the message was there for her to read in his eyes. It wasn't the desperate passion she'd once assumed she wanted, but the love she felt coming from him, his need to have her a part of his life, was far more potent than any action he could have taken, any words he could have said.

Feeling weak with her love, Janine whispered, simply, "Love me, Zach."

Zach's mouth found hers with a sweet desperate ardor. If she was suffering any lingering doubts they vanished like mist in the sun as his lips devoured hers, twisting her into tight knots of desire.

His arms locked around her and he rolled onto his back, pulling her with him so that her softness pressed against the full length of his hard muscular frame. His hands outlined her face as though he half expected her to stop him.

"Make me your wife," she whispered, bending forward to brush her moist mouth over his.

Zach groaned, and then he did the strangest, most wonderful thing. He laughed. The robust sound echoed across the room and was so infectious that it made Janine grin.

"My sweet Janine," he said. "You've lit up my life." And then he kissed her again, leaving her with no doubts at all.

For a long time afterward, their happiness could be heard in their sighs and gasps and whispered words of love....

THE BUZZING SOUND refused to go away. Janine moaned softly and flung out her hand, hoping to find the source of the distraction. But before she could locate it, the noise ceased abruptly.

"Good morning, wife," Zach whispered close to her ear.

Her eyes remained closed as she smiled leisurely. "Good morning, husband." Rolling onto her back, she held her arms open wide to him. "I had the most marvelous dream last night."

Zach chuckled softly. "That wasn't any dream."

"But it must have been," she said, slipping her arms around his neck and smiling lazily. "Nothing could be that incredible in real life."

"I didn't think so, either, but you proved me wrong." He kissed her tenderly, and then so thoroughly that by the time he lifted his head, Janine was breathless.

Slowly, almost against her will, her eyes drifted open. His gaze was dark with desire. "You'll be late for work," she warned him.

His smile filled with sensual laziness. "Who cares?"

"Not me," she murmured. And with a small cry of pleasure, she willingly gave herself to her husband.

Zach was already an hour late for the office when he dragged himself out of bed and headed for the shower. Wearing her husband's pajama top, Janine wandered into the kitchen and prepared a pot of coffee, going through the motions by rote. She leaned her hip against the counter and smiled softly into space, hardly aware of the passage of time.

A few minutes later, or perhaps it was longer, Zach stepped behind her and slid his arms around her waist, nuzzling her neck.

"Zach," she protested, but not too strenuously. She closed her eyes and cradled her arms over his, leaning back against his solid strength. "You're already late."

"I know," he murmured. "If I didn't have an important meeting this morning, I'd skip work altogether."

Twisting around in his arms, Janine tilted back her head to gaze into his eyes. "You'll be home for dinner?"

"Keep looking at me like that and I'll be home for lunch."

Janine smiled. "It's almost that time now."

"I know," he growled, reluctantly pulling away from her. "We'll go out to dinner tonight to celebrate," he said, kissing her again. His mouth was hot on her own, feverish with demand and need and passion. He lifted his head, but his eyes remained shut. "Then we'll come home and celebrate."

Janine sighed. Married life was beginning to agree with her.

At precisely five, Zach was back. He stood just inside the door, loosening his tie, when Janine appeared. A smile traveled to his mouth as their eyes met and held. Neither moved. They stared at each other as if they'd spent years apart instead of a few short hours.

Janine was feeling distinctly light-headed. "Hi," she managed to say, shocked that her voice sounded more like a hoarse whisper than the cheery greeting she'd intended. "How'd the meeting go?"

"Bad."

"Bad?"

He nodded slowly and stepped forward, placing his briefcase on the edge of his desk. "I was supposed to be listening to an important financial report, but unfortunately all I could think about was how much longer the thing would take so I could get back home to my wife."

"Oh." That wasn't the most intelligent bit of conversation she'd ever delivered, but just looking at Zach was enough to wipe out all her normal thought processes.

"It got to be almost embarrassing." His look was intimate and loving as he advanced two more steps toward her. "In the middle of it, I started smiling, and then I embarrassed myself further by laughing outright."

"Laughing? Something was funny?"

"I was thinking about your definition of romance. The tryst on the moors was supplied by your grandfather, the walk along the beach, hand in hand, was supplied by me after the wedding. But the desperate passion, my dear sweet wife, was something we found together."

Her eyes glazed over with moisture.

"Dear sweet heaven, Janine, I love you."

They started toward each other then, but stopped abruptly when the doorbell chimed. Zach's questioning eyes met hers. Janine shrugged, not knowing who it could possibly be.

The second Zach answered the door, Anton flew into the room, looking more determined than Janine had ever seen him.

"All right, you two, sit down," he ordered, waving them in the direction of the sofa.

"Gramps?"

"Anton?"

Janine glanced at Zach, but he looked as mystified as she did. So she just shrugged and complied with her grandfather's demand. Zach sat down next to her.

Gramps paced the carpet directly in front of them, looking thoroughly disgruntled.

"Janine and I had lunch the other day," Anton said, directing his words to Zach. "Two things were made clear to me then. First and foremost she's crazy in love with you, but I doubt she's told you that."

"Gramps—" Janine started, but her grandfather silenced her with a single look.

"The next thing I realized is that she's unhappy. Terribly unhappy. Being in love is difficult enough but—"

"Anton," Zach broke in, "if you'd—"

Gramps cut him off with the same laser-eyed look he'd sent Janine.

"Don't interrupt me, boy. I'm on a roll and I'm not about to stop now. If I noticed Janine was a little melancholy at lunch, it was nothing compared to what I've been noticing about you." Suddenly he ceased his pacing and planted himself squarely in front of Zach. "All week I've been hearing complaints and rumors about you. Folks in the office claim you're there all hours of the day and night, working until you're ready to drop. The fact is, I know you, Zach, probably better than anyone else does. You're in love with my granddaughter, and it's got you all tangled up inside."

"Gramps—"

"Shh." He dismissed Janine with a hard shake of his head. "Now I may be an old man, but I'm not dense. Maybe the way I went about bringing the two of you together wasn't the smartest way, or the conventional way, but by golly it worked." He hesitated long enough to smile proudly. "In the beginning I had my doubts. Janine put up a bit of fuss."

"I believe you said something about how it's easier to pluck a live chicken," Zach inserted, slanting a secret smile at Janine.

"True enough. I never knew that girl had so much spunk. But the fact is, Zachary, as you'll recall, you weren't all that keen on the idea yourself. You both think because I'm retirement age I don't notice things. But I do. You were two lonely people, filling up your lives with unimportant relationships, avoiding love, avoiding life. I care about you. Too damn much to sit back and do nothing."

"It worked out," Janine said, wanting to reassure him.

"At first I thought it had. I arranged the trip to Scotland and it looked like everything was falling neatly into place, like one of those old movie scripts. I couldn't have been more pleased when you announced that you were going to marry. It was sooner than I'd anticipated, but I assumed that meant matters between the two of you were progressing nicely. Apparently I was wrong. Now I'm worried."

"You don't need to be."

"That's not the way I see it," Gramps said with a fierce glare. "Tell him you love him, Janine. Look Zach in the eye and put aside that silly pride of yours. He needs to know it. He needs to hear it. I told you from the first that he wasn't going to be an easy man to know, and that you'd need to be patient with him. What I didn't count on was that damnable pride of yours."

"You want me to tell Zach I love him? Here? Now?"

"Yes!"

Janine turned to her husband and, feeling a little self-conscious, lowered her eyes.

"Tell him," Gramps barked.

"I love you, Zach," she said softly. "I really do."

Gramps gave a loud satisfied sigh. "Good, good. Okay, Zach, it's your turn."

"My turn?"

"Tell Janine what you feel and don't go all arrogant on me."

Zach's hand reached for Janine's. He lifted her palm to his mouth and brushed his lips against the tender skin there. "I love you," he whispered.

"Add something else," Gramps instructed, gesturing toward him. "Something along the lines that you'd be a lost and lonely soul without her. Women like to hear that sort of thing. Damn foolishness, I know, but necessary."

"I'd be a lost and lonely soul without you," Zach repeated, then looked back to Janine's grandfather. "How'd I do?"

"Better than most. Is there anything else you'd like him to say, Janine?"

She released an expressive sigh. "I don't think so."

"Good. Now I want the two of you to kiss."

"Here? In front of you?"

"Yes," Gramps insisted.

Janine slipped into Zach's arms. The smile he shared with her was so devastating that she felt her heart race with anticipation. Her eyes fluttered closed as his mouth settled on hers, thrilling her with promises for all the years to come.

Gently, provocatively, Zach moved his mouth over hers, ending his kiss all too soon to suit Janine. From the shudder that coursed through him, Janine knew it was all too soon to suit him, too. Reluctantly they pulled apart. Zach looked deeply into her eyes, and Janine responded with a soft smile.

"Excellent, excellent."

Janine had all but forgotten her grandfather's presence. When she tore her gaze away from Zach, she discovered Gramps sitting across from them, his hands braced against the arms of the leather chair. He looked exceedingly proud of himself. "Are you two going to be all right now?"

"Yes, sir," Zach answered for them both, his eyes hazy with desire as he smiled at Janine. She could feel herself blushing, and realized her eyes were foggy with the same longing.

"Good!" Gramps declared, nodding once for emphasis. A slow grin overtook his mouth. "I knew all the two of you needed was a little assistance from me." He paused and inhaled deeply. "Since you're both getting along so well, maybe now would be the time to bring up the subject of children."

"Anton," Zach said, slowly rising to his feet. He moved across the room and opened the door. "If you don't mind, I'll take care of that myself."

"Soon?" Gramps wanted to know.

Zach's eyes met Janine's. "Soon," he promised.

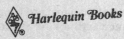

COMING IN 1991 FROM HARLEQUIN SUPERROMANCE:

Three abandoned orphans,
one missing heiress!

Dying millionaire Owen Byrnside receives an
anonymous letter informing him that twenty-six years
ago, his son, Christopher, fathered a daughter. The
infant was abandoned at a foundling home that
subsequently burned to the ground, destroying all
records. Three young women could be Owen's long-
lost granddaughter, and Owen is determined to track
down each of them! Read their stories in

#434 HIGH STAKES (available January 1991)
#438 DARK WATERS (available February 1991)
#442 BRIGHT SECRETS (available March 1991)

Three exciting stories of intrigue and romance by
veteran Superromance author Jane Silverwood.

HARLEQUIN
Romance®

Coming Next Month

#3115 ARROGANT INVADER Jenny Arden
There had never been much love lost between Gwenyth Morgan and
Jeb Hunter, though now he seems determined to pursue her. But since
Gwenyth is happily engaged to Marc and planning a future in France, what is
there to be afraid of?

#3116 LOVE'S AWAKENING Rachel Ford
Just sixteen when she'd been emotionally blackmailed into marrying
Alex Petrides, Selina had run away within hours of the wedding. Alex hadn't
followed as she'd expected. Now, three years later, something irresistibly
draws her back to Greece.

#3117 THE ONLY MAN Rosemary Hammond
Her father's death and her fiancé's jilting leaves Jennie in shock. Then
Alex Knight, her father's friend, gives her a home and a job at his winery. But
Alex treats her as a child when Jennie longs to be recognized as a woman....

#3118 TWO AGAINST LOVE Ellen James
Christie Daniels has just managed to escape one domineering man—her
father—when she's confronted with another. Matt Gallagher's mission is to
talk her into leaving her New Mexico bed-and-breakfast and returning to her
father's brokerage firm in New York City. Christie has no intention of
agreeing, but she *does* wish Matt weren't so darned attractive....

#3119 AN UNCOMMON AFFAIR Leigh Michaels
Marsh Endicott mistakenly thinks Torey Farrell will be pleased to sell him her
half share of the house they jointly inherited. Torey, though, can't wait to
start a new life in the house—and certainly doesn't want a ready-made,
already engaged housemate!

#3120 RITES OF LOVE Rebecca Winters
Courtney Blake, who's half Miccosukee, accuses the man she loves of
betraying the tribe's faith in him. She flees to her mother's family in the
Everglades, but Jonas follows her—and forces her to confront her own lack of
faith in their love.

Available in April wherever paperback books are sold, or through
Harlequin Reader Service:

In the U.S.
P.O. Box 1397
Buffalo, N.Y.
14240-1397

In Canada
P.O. Box 603
Fort Erie, Ontario
L2A 5X3